Revengeful Chatter

When Leslie Cries, Volume 2

Amy Richie

Published by Amy Richie, 2018.

REVENGEFUL CHATTER

First edition. June 15, 2018.

Copyright © 2018 Amy Richie.

ISBN: 979-8227135636

Written by Amy Richie.

Revengeful Chatter
Book Two

"THERE'S BEEN SOME DEVELOPMENTS in your case," Dr. Matthews said slowly, his deep voice vibrating off the walls of his office.

"What developments?" I picked at the strings hanging from the bottom of my pants. They were too big and dragged under my feet when I walked.

"The police have found evidence that links Ethan Sturgis to the night you were attacked."

"So they finally admit that he did it?" I tried not to let my heart react to that.

"Yes."

"Does that mean they're going to let me out of here now?"

"You still killed someone, Mellie. No matter what your reasons were, you can't take the law into your own hands."

"Then what do I care what evidence they found? It makes no difference to me – I already knew Ethan did it."

"It does make a difference though, it affects the court's decision later on how long you have to stay."

"Later?"

"Once we..."

He hesitated but I knew what he wanted to say. "After I get rid of Leslie?"

"Yes."

"What if I like it here, Dr. Matthews?" I leaned back so I could see him better.

"This is not a home or a satisfactory life for a young woman."

"I'm not leaving without Leslie."

Next to me on the couch, Leslie smiled wide at Dr. Matthews. "Who are you to say what is a satisfactory life for Mellie," she scowled, scrunching her nose in distaste. "Me and her are in this thing together so stop trying to make her leave."

"Leslie is in here too?" Dr. Matthews asked, raising both his eyebrows.

"She says it's not a good idea for me to talk to you alone."

Leslie nodded quickly. "You keep trying to make her leave me."

"I'm only doing what is best for Mellie."

"I know what's best for her," Leslie jabbed her finger into her own chest. Her and Dr. Matthews always had this argument.

"This is a break through in your case," Dr. Matthews tried again.

"Not really." I spun the wrapper off a mint and popped the small disc into my mouth. "I'm staying right where I am unless they let Leslie out too. If they can forgive me, they can forgive her too."

"Leslie is dangerous."

She snorted loudly. "I'm only dangerous to people who try to hurt Mellie. I'm only here to protect her."

MY SMILE WOULDN'T BE dulled. I knew I was grinning like a fool but but my lips refused to relax into a straight line.

"You seem happy today," Beth noted, leaning over to speak low in my ear.

"Must be the concert," I whispered back, knowing full well it didn't have much to do with that.

Folded out white chairs were set up in rows behind an old brown piano in the day room. Some lady who claimed to be doing *God's work* was going to come sing for us.

Having something different to listen too was a tiny bit exciting but I knew I was more excited to be able to hang out with Beth.

"Yeah right," she laughed, the sound tickling the hair by my ears. "Is Leslie excited too?"

"She didn't come." It was always awkward to hear Beth talk about Leslie. She accepted her as a part of me, but I couldn't help but know the truth. Leslie wasn't real and Beth couldn't see her.

"Why not?"

"Maybe I wanted to be alone with just you," I teased her, my face flaming hot despite myself. I had to resist my urge to hide my face.

"We're never alone here," Beth rolled her eyes as the chairs slowly filled up around us.

"You guys aren't going to start making out, are you?" Carrie sneered, taking the empty place next to Beth.

"We wouldn't want to make you too jealous," Beth sneered back.

I bit down hard on my bottom lip, really wishing I was as brave as Beth. "Yeah," I squeaked, but she was already turning away so I wasn't sure if she heard me.

"Whatever," she muttered.

"Don't even listen to her," Beth told me, loud enough for Carrie to hear.

"I'm not," I grinned again, my lips pulled ridiculously tight against my teeth.

"I heard this lady is really good, even if all her songs are about church."

"My mom used to make me go to church every week."

"Was it awful?"

I shrugged one shoulder. "It was boring."

"Alright ladies," Nurse Kaydee stepped to the front of the room and clapped her hands loudly. "Listen up."

As one, we turned to look at her.

"You all better be on your best behavior today, I don't want any sort of commotion during the music."

Ever so slowly, with my heart hammering wildly inside my chest, I moved my hand to touch Beth's hand that was laying on my leg. She showed no hesitation to take my hand fully in hers and entwine our fingers. My heart continued to speed along, so loudly I was afraid Nurse Kaydee would consider it a commotion.

"Hello ladies," a very tall woman exclaimed, gliding into the room with her long skirt and frizzy hair.

"Hello," some people murmured back, out of sync.

"I think that you ladies are perfect," she whimpered, templing her fingers under her chin.

There were a few snickers from the crowd. Behind her, Nurse Kaydee rolled her eyes dramatically. I had a feeling that she didn't see us as perfect.

"God made you perfect," the woman continued. "You've just hit some speed bumps." Someone catcalled loudly.

"Alright," Nurse Kaydee called, "you can start the music now." The woman's smile faltered slightly but she obediently moved to the piano and sat down.

"I hope this doesn't suck," Beth whispered.

It didn't really matter what the music sounded like, I thought foolishly. I was just happy to be there. "Me too," I whispered back, giving a small squeeze to her hand.

"TRY THAT ONE," LESLIE suggested, pointing to a blue piece.

"We've already done this puzzle like seventeen times," I reminded her, snatching the suggested piece.

"That's alright," she shrugged, "makes it easier."

"Isn't this kind of cheating?"

Her top lip snarled up. "Who the hell do you think is watching us? Or even cares?"

I glanced behind me at the scattered people that were not looking my way. "I guess you're right."

"So," Leslie leaned back in her chair, "how was the music program yesterday?"

My face immediately felt hot. "It was fine," I croaked.

"Yeah?" Her lips turned up into a crooked smile. "Good music?"

"It was church music."

"So you weren't there for the music."

"Stop trying to embarrass me," I hissed, trying to hide my grin.

"I barely had to try at all," she laughed. "Maybe I should ask Beth what her intentions are here."

"Don't talk to Beth," I warned her, my grin dying fast.

"Why not?"

"I just...I don't..."

"You don't want her to know you're crazy?" Leslie wriggled her eyebrows at me.

"I don't want it to be weird." The words fell out of my mouth in a rush of heat and fluster.

"Why would it be weird?" She stared at me without blinking, waiting for me to explain to her why she wasn't allowed to talk to Beth.

"Leslie..."

"Parker." Nurse Kaydee was suddenly there, looming large over the table.

"Yeah?"

"Who are you talking to?"

"Leslie."

"You see Leslie today?"

"I see her everyday, Nurse Kaydee."

"The doctor needs to adjust your medication. Did you tell him you still see her?"

"Dr. Matthews knows. He can't stop Leslie from coming to me, no medication can if I don't want it too." I smiled lightly, recounting what Dr. Matthews had told me months before.

Nurse Kaydee frowned deeply. "It's not healthy to see people who aren't real."

"She's real to me."

Pressing her lips tight together, she pulled a pen from her pocket and stomped away.

"You know she's gonna write all that down in her notes," Leslie teased, wriggling her eyebrows again.

"YOU GOT MAIL, PARKER," the nurse announced as she unlocked my room door.

"Mail?"

"Someone wrote you a letter," she winked, nodding to the thin envelope on the bed.

Leslie was already sitting in there, peering down at the letter with keen interest. "Who would write to you?" she wondered aloud.

"I don't know." Forehead wrinkled, I snatched the letter up and read the return address. "It's my mom," I scowled.

"You mom?" Leslie bounded up to read the name over my shoulder. "She's never written to you before."

"I know." With narrow eyes, I ripped the top of the envelope and pulled out a single sheet of paper with mom's tidy handwriting on one side.

"Read it out loud," Leslie ordered, settling herself back on the bed.

"Dear Melody," I began, automatically pinching my voice to make it sound more like moms. "How are you doing? Your father and I are doing as well as can be expected, considering the circumstances."

"Circumstances?" Leslie interrupted loudly. "Is she talking about you being in here? Is that what's causing *her* distress?"

Ignoring her, I continued reading. "We have decided to get a divorce. The house is going on the market next month and I'll be getting a small apartment in town. Your father is already moved out. Have Dr. Matthews call me if you need anything. Love, mom."

The paper felt heavy in my hands, everything felt heavy. "A divorce?" I whispered.

"Who would want to be married to that woman anyways," Leslie snorted.

I couldn't laugh though. This was my fault, their lives were falling apart because of what I had done. Last time she had visited, mom had told Dr. Matthews that she couldn't even go to the grocery store without someone saying something to her about me. And she didn't want to move in case I needed her. Maybe she didn't hate me as much as I thought.

Well – she would now.

"MY MOM WROTE ME A LETTER," I said slowly, carefully keeping my eyes on the dingy ceiling above me and Beth.

"I'm guessing it wasn't cheerful?"

"Good guess."

There was a wooden door in the cafeteria that led to an old part of the hospital that had been closed off years before either of us had gotten there. The nurses told Beth it was creepy but the short hallway just off a large, dusty room was the perfect hiding place. And since day room time followed lunch on Tuesdays and Thursdays, those days had become my favorite times of the week. Beth and I could hide out back there for at least an hour and no one noticed.

Or maybe they just didn't care.

"What did she say?" Beth questioned in a low voice.

"My parents are getting divorced."

"Is that good or bad?"

"I don't know," I confessed. "Me being in here must be hard on them."

"Probably."

"How long do you think I've been here?"

"A few weeks?"

"It's been longer than that," I scoffed, rolling my eyes.

Beth chuckled lightly. "Didn't you just have a birthday?"

"I turned 21," I nodded. It wasn't much of a birthday celebration, but she was right.

"So that means you've been here for two years."

"No way." Was it even possible that I had been there that long? "I don't think it's been that long."

"It's those pills." She jabbed my side with one finger. "They make you forget stuff."

"Two years though," I sighed deeply. No wonder mom was taking things so hard, she had been waiting a long time for me to get better. "Unreal."

"At least we're here together."

I turned my head, meeting her smile with one of my own. "Yes, at least there's that."

"MELLIE," BETH KICKED my shin underneath the small square table sitting against the wall of the day room.

"What?" My eyes jerked to look back at her.

"What are you looking at over there?" She turned to look at the empty place that drew my attention.

It wasn't empty to me though. Leslie sat cross legged on top of a table, glaring at me from across the room. I knew she was mad at me for not letting her sit with us, but I wasn't changing my mind. She wasn't allowed to talk to Beth and that was final. I was the one in charge here; Leslie was just my imaginary friend.

My nerves were on high alert though.

"I'm not looking at anything," I smiled at Beth and took my turn on the checkered board. I couldn't stop myself from jumping when Leslie smacked the table with the palm of her hand.

"Are you sure you're alright?" Beth laid her hand on my arm near my elbow.

"Yeah," I shook her hand away. "Your move."

She slid a rook forward three squares. "Is Leslie over there?" she asked quietly.

My teeth clenched together, of course she knew. "She's mad."

"Why is she mad?"

"I just..." My tongue slid slowly over my bottom lip and then back into my mouth. "I don't want her to talk to you."

"I don't mind talking to her," she shrugged.

My breath sucked in sharply and then cut off. She didn't mind? That meant she had already talked to her. How often did they talk? What did they talk about? I wanted to demand the answers, but my voice was gone completely. Maybe I didn't really want to know anyways. Silent and angry, I slid my queen forward.

"DID YOU WIN?" LESLIE smiled but her lips were too tight to be considered friendly.

"We don't play to win."

"What?"

"I don't even know how to play chess."

"So you just sit and push the pieces around the board with no purpose?"

"Do you know how to play?" I frowned at her.

"Yeah."

"How?"

"Beth taught me."

There it was again, the insinuation that she had talked to Beth more than I liked to think about. "She did?"

"It was before you told me not to talk to her." She smiled that same smile, the unhappy one.

"I told you why I didn't."

"Whatever." She pulled her legs underneath her on the floor and leaned her head back against the wall. "I don't know why you like her so much."

I didn't know how to explain to Leslie why I liked Beth so much. She was the only person I had ever met that accepted me just the way I was. She never asked me to change, and yet because of her I had changed so much.

When I looked in the mirror these days, I hardly recognized the person I saw there. Leslie said it was the hospital that was changing me, but I didn't exactly hate this new version of myself.

Settling under my covers, I glanced over at Leslie. Maybe it's because she's pretty," I teased, grinning in the darkness.

"You always like the pretty ones," Leslie scowled, her tight face relaxing some.

Giggles erupted from my throat. "There's nothing wrong with that."

"If she makes you happy, I'll never say a bad thing about her."

"She does." I rolled over to my back and continued smiling at the ceiling. "I like the way she smells."

Leslie laughed loudly.

IT WAS TUESDAY, ONE of my favorite days of the week.

I was surprised that it wasn't Nurse Kaydee who came to take me to lunch, a man stood at the doorway – angry and frowning. "Lunch," he growled.

"Where is Nurse Kaydee?"

"Get you ass out here."

Shocked, I just stood there.

"Do I need to come in there and get you?" he asked, raising both eyebrows high on his head.

"Who the hell does he think he is?" Leslie hissed from behind my right shoulder.

"Shhh," I elbowed her back. She was going to get us both in trouble and I didn't want to miss lunch today.

"What was that?" His lips tightened into a thick line, slightly puckered at the corners.

"Nothing." I scurried froward to follow him down the hallway that led to the cafeteria.

"No talking," he ordered once we reached the full room.

I swallowed hard, trying to understand. Why was it so much fuller than usual? Why wasn't I allowed to talk? Where was Nurse Kaydee? I needed to find Beth, she would know what was going on. The nurses liked her and told her things the rest of us didn't know.

"He can't tell you what to do," Leslie scowled, sliding in front of me at the table. "Don't listen to him."

"I have to listen to him," I whispered, glancing around to see where he went. There were at least half a dozen angry men in the cafeteria, standing against the walls and watching us as we ate. They didn't speak to each other or to any of the nurses that fluttered around the tables, looking as scared as I felt. "What's going on, Leslie? I don't see Beth anywhere."

"I don't know," she frowned, "but I don't like it."

"BACK INSIDE," THE SAME man that had led me to lunch, led me back to my room directly after I ate.

"It's day room time," I protested.

"Not today."

"Don't talk to her that way," Leslie growled in the same tone he used.

His eyes widened and then narrowed almost immediately. "What did you say to me?"

Alarmed, I wanted to take a step back but I wasn't sure I would be allowed to. "I didn't say anything."

"I did," Leslie pushed ahead of me so she could angrily face him.

"I hate crazy prisoners," he sneered, not bothering to disguise his contempt. "They make my head hurt, so just keep your mouth shut and do what you're told."

"I..."

"In your cell," he repeated loudly, swinging is arm to help me along.

With no choice that I could see, I trudged slowly back into the room. The door was shut promptly behind me. "Am I going to see Dr. Matthews?" I asked him through the small barred window.

"Only allowed out at meal times." Then he slammed the window closed and left me to my own silence.

TAKING A DEEP BREATH, I did a quick scan of the day room. It was already almost full but Beth was noticeably missing – or maybe I was the only one who noticed.

"Go sit down," Nurse Kaydee ordered gently.

"Where's Beth," I asked her in a low hiss. I was all too aware of the new male guards that were positioned inside the room.

This was the first time we had been allowed to go to the day room in weeks and I didn't like the new additions. "Go on in," Nurse Kaydee pushed me lightly through the wide door.

I hurried to an empty table and sank down on the wooden chair. Leslie leaned against the wall nearby, glaring at the silent guard across the room.

"Why are they here?" Leslie asked loudly.

"One of the nurses was killed," a short girl with frizzy black hair responded smugly.

"What?"

The girl, called Janice, sauntered over to my table and slid into the other chair. "Your girlfriend, Beth, did it."

My chest felt like it had been punched, fear began to claw it's way up into my voice. "What are you talking about?" I managed to get out.

"Two weeks ago," Janice shrugged. "That's why we've all been on lock down."

"A nurse was killed?" My eyes narrowed, searching for a lie. "How do you know?"

"Heard the nurses talking. She was found with like ten needles in her legs and her wrists slit."

"Maybe she did it to herself." Why was my mouth going so dry?

"She was killed. By Beth."

"Beth would never kill someone."

"She already has."

"That's not true." My chest heaved with emotion.

"What do you think we're all in here for?" she snorted. "Ward five – crazy killer girls."

"Beth didn't kill anyone." She would have told me.

"That's what we all say." She traced her finger lazily along a mark on the table.

"No."

"Did you kill that boy?" she asked me with a grin.

"I didn't do it; Leslie did."

"And I didn't push my dad down the steps – he fell. And Carrie didn't set the house on fire with her stepbrother inside."

"Shut up, Janice," Carrie flared, throwing a chess piece at her. "You don't know shit about me."

"Settle down," the guard yelled at Carrie.

"Tell her to stop talking about me," Carrie shrilled back, pointing at Janice.

"Do you want to go back to your room?"

"No," she sulked, crossing her arms tightly over her chest.

"Not one of us did it," Janice said again. "Except Beth; she killed the nurse."

I couldn't believe it, no way could Beth kill someone. Mouth still agape, I looked to Leslie. She was still glaring at the guard.

"I UNDERSTAND THAT THIS has been a difficult time for you," Dr. Matthews said gently.

My back teeth were clenched, holding in my screams. Difficult time? Is that really how he saw all this? I twisted my hands in my lap tightly. "Yeah," I muttered, not trusting myself to say anything else.

"It must be scary," he prodded.

"Beth didn't do this," I blurted. "There's no way she did this."

"I understand the two of you were friends?"

"We *are* friends." Heat fanned out across my cheeks. "Where is she?"

"She is confined to her room for now."

"For how long?"

"Until we learn more about why this happened."

"Are you looking for the person that actually killed that nurse – if anyone really did." I still wasn't convinced she hadn't done it to herself.

"Let's talk about how this incident makes you feel," Dr. Matthews suggested, tapping his pen on the notebook.

"I don't want to talk about how I feel." I stood up abruptly and moved to the window. "How did this happen?"

"Harsh reality of a place like this," he said sadly. "This hospital is not a place you should become content in. It's not a home – it's a prison."

I swallowed hard but didn't turn to look at him. Outside, several stories down, was the parking lot. I watched two nurses that I didn't recognize walk to a white car and get inside. The car backed up and pulled away from the hospital. For the first time in a long time, I wished I was leaving too.

"HOW WAS IT WITH THE doctor?" Leslie interrogated me back in my room.

"Fine," I shrugged.

"I still don't understand why you didn't want me to come with you," she pouted.

"I already told you," I sighed. "I wanted him to tell me about Beth."

"He could have told you with me there."

"You already know that Dr. Matthews doesn't like you." I parted my hair into three strands and braided it quickly. I wasn't allowed to have a hair tie in my room so I had to just let it come undone again.

"I don't like him either," she huffed.

"Another reason I didn't want you in there."

"Did he tell you what happened?"

"No." I settled myself on the bed with my legs pulled under me. "Not really."

"Meaning?"

"He said Beth was locked in her room."

"They wouldn't lock her in her room if they didn't have some kind of evidence that she did it."

"I still can't believe Beth would kill someone. She's too nice."

"I think we're missing the most important question."

"Which is?"

"Why did she do it?"

I chewed furiously at the frayed skin on the inside of my cheek. If Beth did kill a nurse, which I still didn't believe, then Leslie was right. What had pushed her to do something like that? It was too much – all too much.

"THIS IS A SAFE CIRCLE," Dr. Carol announced, spinning her finger in a tight circle in front of her, indicating the circle of chairs we were all sitting in. "Inside this circle, you can say what ever you are feeling."

I wasn't the only one to roll my eyes. She said the same thing every single week. And every week, she sounded just as stupid.

"We're going to do things a little differently today," she told us. "We're going to talk about what happened to Nurse Lee."

A murmur of excitement sped through the group.

"I want everyone to say how they feel about what happened. Are you scared?"

"Of course we're scared," Janice scowled. "One of the nurses is dead now. What if it's one of us next?"

"Can that happen?" a young girl asked, fear obvious.

"Beth killed her, are you guys gonna make her leave?"

"How do you know she did it?" I fired at the girl. I had never talked to her before but I wasn't going to just let her speak bad about Beth like that.

"Of course she did it," Carrie snarled. "She's the only one not here."

"That doesn't mean she did it; that just means they have her locked up somewhere."

"Ladies," Dr. Carol attempted to call the circle to order, "we're not here to talk about Beth."

"You said we could talk about it."

"How does it make you feel, Carrie?" She honed her gaze directly on the thin girl.

Carrie took a deep breath that made her shoulders raise up, then let it out slowly. "I don't really care," she finally declared.

"You don't?"

"Nope," her lips popped on the word. "Nurse Lee probably had it coming. She was always such a bitch."

"What about you, Janice? How do you feel?"

"Lock a bunch of crazy girls up in one place – someone is bound to get killed."

"Speak for yourself, Janice," Carrie sneered. "I'm not crazy."

"Let's move on to Mellie," Dr. Carol spoke up over Carrie. "How do you feel Mellie?"

As always, I hated it when the attention was all on me. My face quickly grew hot. "I don't like it."

"You don't like that Nurse Lee was killed?"

"I don't like that Beth is being blamed for something she didn't do."

"Beth was your friend?"

"Her girlfriend," Carrie snickered.

"She didn't do it," I repeated angrily.

"That will be up to the police and the doctors to determine."

"It's not fair. No one will believe her." My throat stung.

"Are you afraid?"

"No."

But Leslie was shaking her head, her shoulders quivering with silent laughter. "That's a lie, Mellie," she trilled.

"It's not completely a lie," I denied. "I'm not afraid of Beth."

"Then what are you afraid of?" Dr. Carol asked softly.

"I'm afraid of this place, I'm afraid of what happens here. And..." I hesitated, my eyes straying to Leslie.

"And what?"

"And, I want to go home," I finally admitted.

"WHY WOULD YOU SAY YOU want to go home?" Leslie whispered in the darkness of the room.

"It just came out."

"Do you want to leave me, Mellie?" She laid beside me on the bed but I refused to look at her.

"No."

"Then?"

"I wish you could come home with me."

"Dr. Matthews isn't going to let me leave this hospital."

"I know." I rubbed my hand roughly over my mouth. "I know he won't."

"But you still want to leave?"

"No," I sighed, "I want to stay with you."

She nodded but didn't smile. "What we need to do is talk to Beth."

"What?" Shocked, I turned to look at her.

"If we talk to her, we can just ask her if she did it or not."

"How can we talk to her? She's not allowed out of her room."

"Isn't it obvious," she asked quietly, "we'll have to go to her."

"How? We're not allowed in other people's rooms."

"Don't worry, Mellie. I have a plan."

IT WAS THURSDAY AND the palms of my hands felt clammy with moisture. "Breathe normal," Leslie hissed in my ear as I carried my lunch tray past an enormous guard.

"Should I smile at him?" I tried to whisper back.

"Keep walking," the guard answered instead of Leslie.

"Take that as a no," I muttered under my breath, sliding onto an empty bench.

"Don't sit there," Leslie scowled. "Get closer to the door."

Despite the disapproving glare from the guard, I rose from the table and found another one at the back of the room. The old wooden door was barely two feet away from me.

It was difficult to eat, I wasn't even sure what kind of meat was sandwiched between the two pieces of over sized bread. The food kept getting stuck in my throat, but I continued eating so I wouldn't draw any attention from the nurses.

"You got one chance at this," Leslie reminded me, looking as tense as my stomach felt.

"I know."

"Don't speak out loud anymore."

"Ok." I pressed my lips tight together to stop anymore words from slipping out.

The guards that stood along the walls were going to make it harder to sneak into the abandoned hallway. As soon as the first few people began to get up from the tables, I ducked under my own table and crawled all the way to the end so I could be closer to the door.

"Just wait," Leslie breathed into my ear. "Wait until everyone leaves."

My heart hammering wildly, I crouched and watched all the legs passing by my table. The nurses were by the doors, ushering people out with the guards. If they decided to come this way at all, they would see me for sure. All I could do was stay where I was and hope for the best.

"I think everyone is gone," Leslie whispered after several moments of silence had passed.

I shrugged, still nervous about making any noise.

"I'm gonna look." I wanted to pull her back down but I didn't move as Leslie peered over the top of the table. "All clear," she announced.

Although my legs were shaking like crazy, I managed to scoot out from under the table and darted the short distance to the unlocked wooden door. It was with very little relief that I slid to the floor and pulled my knees up to my chest.

"Now we just wait until they turn the lights out in the cafeteria," Leslie reminded me, peering out the cracked door.

"You sure that will be enough time for everyone to get to the day room?"

"Yeah." She came to sit next to me, relaxed and serious. "Beth's room is further down the hall than yours from the day room so it will be close to the cafeteria."

"521" I nodded, remembering what Leslie had told me the night before. "Probably past the cafeteria."

"Right."

"Do you think she's scared?"

Lines appeared on her forehead. "I don't know."

It wasn't going to be easy to see Beth locked away like an animal and not be able to do anything to help her. Who was I though? I was just another crazy killer girl, trying to save her girlfriend. No one was going to believe a thing I said either. Maybe seeing Beth would only make me feel worse, maybe this wasn't such a good idea.

"Stop thinking so much," Leslie tapped my slippered foot with her shoe.

"I'm not," I lied.

"Lights out."

My heart sped up.

"It's show time."

Those words were like a shot to my already nervous system. I shot up to my feet and slipped out the door into the surprisingly dark cafeteria. Leslie stayed right next to me as I made my way to the double doors that led to the hallway of rooms. Instead of turning towards the day room, I went the other way – hopefully towards room 521, where Beth was being held.

"521," I panted, coming to a stop in front of a door I had never seen before but it looked exactly like my own. "It's here."

"Hurry up and talk to her," Leslie urged, "before we get caught."

"Right." I lurched up to the small, barred window near the top of the door and peered inside. "It's empty," I realized out loud. "Beth isn't in here."

"HEY." I WAS NERVOUS, I felt it all the way to the tips of my fingers. I knew my eyes would be bright and my breathing was too heavy but I couldn't calm myself down. "Janice, can we talk?" Without waiting for her response, I sat across from her in the day room.

"What's up, Mellie?" she asked slowly, shuffling a worn deck of cards.

"Go away," I told the girl sitting at the table with us. "Now."

"Whatever," the girl rolled her eyes but thankfully obeyed.

"You're late at joining us in here today," Janice noted, glancing over my shoulder at the ruffled nurse I had practically bowled over in my hurry to get in.

"I had to pee," I recited the same lie to her as I had to the nurse when she asked where I'd been.

"You'll be lucky if they don't throw you in the hole." She clicked her tongue against the roof of her mouth.

"They have more important things to worry about right now."

"So, what's on your mind?"

"Beth isn't in her room," I blurted out, practically yelling it for the whole room to hear.

"And you would know this how?"

"It doesn't matter."

"Why are you telling me this?" She began to lay the cards out on the table. "I don't care."

"Because I need your help."

"Can't."

"Where is she?"

"How the hell am I supposed to know?"

"You know everything."

Driving me even crazier than I already was, she slowly and deliberately moved several cards around on the table before responding. "She's probably in the hole, in solitary."

My eyes slid briefly closed. "Of course," I whispered. "I need to see her."

"How ya gonna do that?"

"You can help me."

"But I'm not going to."

"Please," my voice shook.

"Such a pretty girl," she grinned up at me. "You must be used to getting your way with that little whimper of yours."

"No," I said tightly.

"But I'm not gonna give you your way."

"Janice."

"I can't help you."

"I know you can." Desperation clawed at my throat.

Janice leaned back in her seat. "Fine, I'll help."

"You will?"

"But I want something from you."

My eyebrows immediately dropped. "What do you want?"

"I want your hair."

"My hair?"

"Yes." She grinned wider.

"Why do you want my hair?"

"It doesn't matter why I want it, the question is...are you willing to give it to me to see Beth?"

"How can I give you my hair?"

"Just cut it off and put it all in a plastic bag."

"I'm not cutting my hair."

"Then I'm not helping you." She turned her attention back to her cards.

I bit hard on my lip to stop it from shaking. "You're a crazy bitch," I fired at her, sweeping my arm across the table and sending her cards flying everywhere.

Janice threw back her head and laughed.

"YOU HAVEN'T BEEN SLEEPING." It wasn't a question, it was an observation. Dr. Matthews studied me with wise and knowing eyes. "Have you been taking your medication?"

"The nurses make me," I replied shortly, chewing relentlessly on the frayed skin on the side of my thumb.

"You need to sleep at night."

"They can't force me to sleep," I half growled. "You can shove all the little white pills down my throat that as you want, you're not going to fix me."

"Is that Leslie speaking, or you?"

"Leslie isn't here." Wasn't it obvious to him that she had stopped coming with me to these meetings? Wasn't he the one with all the framed sheets of paper hanging on his office wall? He should know these things.

"Did she not want to come?"

"I know you don't like her," I pulled my knee close to my chest. "And I know that if she comes, you won't be able to talk to me."

"What would you like to talk about?"

"Beth."

Although his expression didn't change drastically, I saw him straighten slightly in his seat and sit back to look at me more carefully. This was his worried face. "Ok," he said slowly.

"Where is she?" My knee dropped so I could lean closer to him. "And don't tell me she's in her room because I know she isn't."

"How do you know she isn't?" he asked calmly. It didn't escape my notice that he wasn't denying it.

"I went and looked." My leg jerked at the confession. I already knew that the things we talked about, he wasn't allowed to tell anyone else but I couldn't hide my nerves.

"How?"

"After lunch." Telling him I went was one thing, but I wasn't giving up the secret hallway. "So I know she isn't in there," I held my arms out in front of me to stop him from asking any more about how I had managed my illegal visit. "Where is she?"

Dr. Matthews took his time answering and his lips moved silently the entire time, as if he were chewing on the truth and trying to decide if he should give it to me or not. "She's being securely held," he finally said out loud.

"What does that mean?"

"Mellie, I'm sure you remember that this place is more than a hospital. It's a prison as well, only those that have broken the law in a severe way are held here."

"Yeah," I snapped, impatient.

"Killing a nurse is a very serious thing."

"Why are you talking to me like I'm stupid?" I smacked the palm of my hand against the couch. "I know murder is serious. I'm not stupid."

"Then you understand why she is being held in a secure location for now."

"No, I don't understand it," I fired angrily. "Beth did not kill anyone."

"Unfortunately..."

"Wait," I cut him off with another wild swing of my arm, "what do you mean for now? Are you letting her out? Or will you send her away?"

"Unfortunately," he began again as if I hadn't cut him off, "I am unable to disclose any confidential information regarding Beth or the accusations against her."

"That's horse shit!" The words exploded out of me without any thought. "You're going to send her away, aren't you?"

"How would that make you feel?"

"Where will she go? This is her home." Tears cracked my voice, threading my words together in a mushy declaration.

"This is not a home," he repeated patiently.

"Can I see her?"

"That's not possible."

"Please. Just let me see her for like two minutes."

Dr. Matthews scribbled across his notebook and then turned back to me, his lips turned down. "I know this is very difficult for you."

Realizing I had lost him, I leaned back on the couch and brought both knees against my chest. "Horse shit," I muttered under my breath, not bothering to wipe away my tears.

"WHAT SHOULD I DO?" I asked quietly. The lights had gone out a while before, but my eyes wouldn't stay closed. Leslie sat on the edge of the bed, cross legged and deep in thought.

"You have to see Beth before they move her." She stated the obvious.

"Dr. Matthews won't let me." I also stated the obvious.

"Janice can get you in to see her."

"She's crazy."

"We're all crazy," she reminded me in a hollow sort of way.

"Yeah." My sigh was too heavy, mom would have never approved.

"You have to decide what is more important to you. Your hair," she held up one hand, palm side up, "or seeing Beth again," she held up the other hand.

I tapped the hand that indicated Beth. "I need to see her."

She closed the hand that stood for my hair and brought the fist close to her chest. "It's only hair," she pointed out.

"But it's finally long."

"It'll grow back."

Leslie was right, as usual. If that was the only way for me to see Beth, then that was what I was going to do. I'd cut my hair off and give it to Janice. Why did she even want it? I shuddered in the darkness, not even wanting to know the answer.

"How will I even do it?" I wondered out loud after a long stretch of silence. "It's not like the nurses are going to let me borrow their scissors."

"Don't you worry," Leslie grinned, "I have a plan."

I smiled up at the ceiling; I knew all along that Leslie would know what to do. Still, I couldn't completely rid myself of the remorse over losing my hair. Oh well, I mentally shrugged, mom had always said I didn't look good with long hair.

"OK," I TOLD JANICE on a huff. "I'll do it."

Pursing her lips, she glared up at me. "You'll give me your hair?"

"Obviously," I snarled. Why did she have to look so pleased about it? It was weird, and my face couldn't disguise how I felt about her. Still, I needed her. "But I need your help to get some scissors."

"That's easy." She was smiling wide now, her face creased with obvious smugness.

"The nurses aren't going to just give me scissors," I pointed out.

"You're not going to ask them," she snorted. "Why do I have to tell you everything?"

"I wasn't planning on asking, Janice." It was hard not to spit her name out on the table between us. She wasn't a nice girl; under normal circumstances, I wouldn't have even said hello to her. If I was being honest with myself, I was more than just a little afraid of her.

"The scissors are kept in the second drawer in the cart over there," she nodded towards the nurse's cart without actually looking at it or making it obvious.

I had seen them give plenty of stitches in the day room so I knew they had a small pair in there. Of course Janice would know exactly where they were. "They never leave that cart though," I hissed.

"I'll create a diversion."

"How?"

"Don't worry about that. All you need to worry about is getting those scissors."

"Whatever." I leaned back and crossed my arms over my chest.

"Go sit on the couch," she ordered. "It's closest to the cart."

I wanted to argue, but she was right. Anyways, I didn't object to getting further away from her. Arms still crossed, I sulked over to the couch and plopped onto an empty cushion and waited. I wasn't even sure what I was waiting for – diversion could have meant anything. Just when I was starting to think Janice was full of crap, it happened.

"What are you doing?" Someone screeched.

Instinctively, I moved with everyone else to see what had happened. Janice was flopping around on the floor, smacking her face hard every time she flopped back down.

"Something is wrong with Janice," Carrie yelled at the nurse. "She's dying. Someone else is dying."

"Move back," Nurse Kaydee thundered, pushing the crowd out of her way to get to Janice. "I said move!"

For a moment I just stood there, not sure what was going on. Then I turned around and realized that the cart was left unattended. In their hurry to get to Janice, the nurses had left their cart. This was my chance.

With plenty of nervous energy, I ran to the cart and ripped open the second drawer. I almost cried when I saw the small silver scissors. Scooping them up, I shoved them into the waistband of my pants in the same movement and slammed the drawer shut again. My heart was hammering when I sat back on the couch and tried to pretend everything was normal.

"HERE," LESLIE THREW an empty garbage bag onto the bed beside me.

"What's this?"

"Garbage bag," she grunted.

"I see that." I touched the rough plastic with one finger. "But where did you get it?"

"I took it from the day room before we left," she shrugged. "I knew you would need something to put your hair into after..."

"After I cut it off," I finished hollowly.

"Yeah."

I brought the scissors out from where I had stowed them under my mattress. "Should I cut it all off?"

"Might as well do as much as possible," Leslie frowned. "You don't want crazy Janice to say that it isn't enough."

"Do you think she really can help me see Beth?"

"Yeah, she always seems to know everything around here."

That was true. Even Beth had told me that if I ever wanted anything, Janice was the girl to get it for you – and she was terrified of Janice. Thinking of Beth strengthened my wavering resolve.

The scissors were the tiny ones that they used to cut bandages so I knew it would take a long time to cut all my thick hair off, and I had to do it in between bed checks.

"Just hurry up and do it," Leslie coaxed as I hesitated, scissors held against my hair.

"I don't know if I can," I admitted in a small voice. "My hands are shaking too much."

"Do you want me to do it?"

"Will you?" I squeezed my eyes shut tight.

My heart slammed against my ribs as the sound of the metal on the scissor blades scrapped against each other. "There," Leslie declared, "The first cut is made. No going back now."

Nodding, I took the scissors from her and continued cutting.

"TIME TO GET UP," NURSE Kaydee barked, flipping the light on. "Out of bed."

"Mmm," I groaned, kicking my feet wildly to stop her from pulling on them like she did every single morning.

"Come on, sleepy head," she growled with a hint of playfulness. Nurse Kaydee was harsh and strict, but she had a kindness to her that emerged after a long time of being there with her. Or maybe Leslie was right and she just had a crush on me.

"Ten more minutes," I whined, knowing she would say no.

"Nope!" Her cold fingers found my toes and pulled lightly. "Hurry up or your oatmeal will get cold."

"Oh no," I moaned dramatically, "not cold oatmeal." Still, I threw the blanket off of me and sat up on the edge of the bed. "I'm sure it wouldn't taste any different."

I glanced up and was slightly stunned to see the look of shock on Nurse Kaydee's face. "What have you done?" she whispered.

"I'm...I'm up," I stammered.

"What happened to your hair?" Her mouth was still hanging open.

"Oh." I tugged lightly on the short strands above my ears. "I cut it."

"How?" Her mouth finally closed, all the way closed until it was just a solid angry line on her face.

"Ummm..."

"Tell her you pulled it out," Leslie hissed.

"I pulled it out."

"That's funny," she fumed, "it looks like you cut it to me."

"No."

"On your feet," she commanded harshly. I obeyed without hesitation. "Give me the scissors."

"I don't have any scissors."

"Make this easy on yourself and give them to me."

"No." I sucked in my lips, refusing to say anymore.

"Why do you always have to do things the hard way?" she snarled before storming out of the room.

Leslie stood next to me. Although she was silent, it was nice to have her there. "What do you think she's gonna do?" I whispered. Leslie just shook her head, whether because she didn't know or because she wanted me to be quiet – I wasn't sure.

"Guard entering," a deep voice suddenly boomed out, followed closely by the guard himself. "Do you have a pair of scissors?" he thundered, looking ready to punch me in the face.

"No," I replied through clenched teeth.

"You understand that you will now be searched?"

"Searched?" I glanced between his face and the face of Nurse Kaydee, both looked angry and pinched.

"If you don't willingly give up your weapon, you will be searched."

"I don't have any weapons," I screeched. "So search all you want."

"Back up," he yelled without taking his eyes off of me.

"What?"

Two more guards came into the room, one of them coming to me and pulling me to the side. His fingers dug into my arms that he held behind my back. "Don't move," he ordered roughly.

"I wasn't planning on it," I growled back. "Even if I could." The second I tried to pull away from him, his grip tightened painfully.

The other two men began pulling my small room apart. The pillow and blanket were stripped from the bed and thrown onto the floor, the trash can was tipped over, the small desk was turned on its side and the few books I had crashed around it, letters from my mom fluttered next to them. Finally, in the tub that held my toothbrush and comb, he found the small pair of silver scissors.

"Weapon found," he announced loudly to the small group.

"That's not a weapon," I denied. "Just scissors."

"This could be used as a weapon."

"I cut my hair with them." Obviously. "It's my hair, I can do what I want with it."

"If you want your hair cut," Nurse Kaydee fired, "you fill out a request form like everyone else."

"Too late," I shrugged.

"Take her out."

"HOW LONG CAN THEY KEEP you in here?" Leslie wondered out loud for both of us.

"They called those scissors a weapon," I scowled, smacking the soft wall lightly with the palm of my hand. "That was a lie though, Nurse Kaydee knows I only took them to cut my hair."

"But she doesn't know you did it to see Beth."

"Yeah and the longer I'm here, the more chance there is for them to send her away before I can see her." Locked down in solitary was never easy, but this was so much worse. The waiting was harder when I was impatient to see Beth before it was too late.

"It's only been a few days," Leslie reminded me, letting her head fall back against the wall. "And they can't keep you here forever."

It didn't matter. No matter how long they kept me locked up in this tiny room, it was worth it. I needed to see Beth and the only way I could do that was to get help from Janice – and she wanted my hair. "Why do you think she wants my hair?"

"No clue." Leslie chuckled lightly, the sound strange in solitary. Any laughter in a place like this was bound to sound crazy. Leslie laughed again.

"I'm really glad they didn't find that bag." I wasn't even that sorry I was in solitary, as long as they didn't find that.

"I told you they wouldn't think to look behind the brick," Leslie grinned.

We had found a loose brick on the floor under the bed. When we pulled it out, there was a small space that was perfect to hide things in. Many sleeping pills had been shoved into that hole and now my hair was stowed safely away. "As soon as I get out of here, I'll give it to Janice so she can take me to Beth."

"It's a pretty good trade," Leslie noted, echoing my own thoughts.

"DID YOU WANT THE SCISSORS for protection?" Dr. Matthews asked, yet again.

"No."

"Why would you want to cut your hair off, Mellie?" He really looked like he was trying to understand. "You've always wanted long hair."

"I changed my mind."

"So you stole the scissors off the nurse cart?"

"Yep."

"Did someone help you?"

"Don't tell him anything," Leslie hissed.

"I already know not to tell him," I whispered back.

"Leslie is here with us today." Dr. Matthews observed.

My eyebrows furrowed, making my forehead wrinkle. Had I spoken too loud to her? Did Dr. Matthews hear what I said? "She decided to come today," I said slowly.

"Was she the one who told you to cut your hair?"

"No." Why would Leslie want me to cut my hair off?

"Then who told you to?"

"No one. I decided that I wanted to, so I did."

"Losing Beth has been a hard blow for you, hasn't it?" His voice dripped with authentic sympathy.

"She made the days easier."

"Tell me about Beth."

"You already know her."

"Yes, but tell me how you saw her."

"Beth is my friend," I sniffed. "I miss playing games with her in the day room and I miss hearing her laugh."

"And?"

"And I'm worried that I won't see her again." My eyes stung with tears, but I didn't let them fall. "I just want to know if she's ok."

"JUST ACT CALM," LESLIE breathed close to my ear. "They'll be watching you closer so you have to act normal."

"I know," I nodded quickly.

"Find a table," the guard barked, tilting his chin towards the cafeteria.

"I am," I snarled back, lifting my top lip at him, but still moving in case he decided to throw me back in solitary.

Since my session with Dr. Matthews had run over, the cafeteria was almost empty by the time I got there. I had hoped to see Janice in there so I could hurry up and get the hair safely to her. I had tucked the bag under my bra just before heading down for lunch. It crinkled when I walked but so far, no one had noticed.

Finding an empty table easily, I dropped my tray down and sat on the bench. The food was never very good here but today I barely even tasted anything. I was in too much of a hurry to get to the day room. My skin felt itchy, my heart was beating too fast. A thin sheen of sweat had broken out on my forehead.

"Act normal," Leslie told me again. "Don't give them a reason to check you."

"I'm trying."

"Eat."

I brought the fork to my lips and shoved the food into my mouth, chewing without tasting.

"I HAVE IT," I HISSED across the table as soon as my butt hit the chair across from Janice.

"Have what?" she snarled, staring fully at me.

"My hair."

"You look like shit."

"I don't care," I snarled back. "I have it though."

"Where is it?"

"In my bra."

"Why?" Her eyes moved to take in my padded chest. "Didn't you think you'd get caught with it there?"

I shrugged, making my eyes go narrow. "No one checked."

"You are so insane."

"So they tell me." I had gotten this far and done this much to ensure Janice was paid, I wasn't sure now how I was going to get it out of my bra and to her. "Is the nurse watching?"

She craned her eyes to see behind me. "No, she's not facing this way. Hurry up."

As quickly as possible, I reached up my shirt and tugged the bag of hair from my bra and slapped it on the table. "There." My tongue slid nervously across my bottom lip. "Now will you help me see Beth?"

"I told you I would," she nodded. Her smile grew wide as she scooped the bag off the table and shoved it into the waist band of her pants.

"How? When?"

"Tonight."

"How?"

"Someone will come to your room for you, just follow him."

"Who will come to my room?"

"Don't worry about it," she snapped. "Just trust me."

But I didn't trust Janice at all, not even a little bit. She lied about everything, or maybe she lied about nothing. Beth didn't like her though and that was enough for me. The problem was – I didn't have any choice but to trust her now.

"WHEN DID SHE SAY HE was coming?" Leslie asked, peeking out the small window on the door.

"She just said to wait for him," I mumbled through my arm that I had draped over my face. There was no point to pace the small room or sit on the edge of my bed to wait for him; neither of those things would make him come any faster.

"I didn't even know there were male nurses here."

"Maybe it's a guard," I pointed out.

"Why would a guard help any of us?"

"A nurse wouldn't help us either though." No one would. We were nothing to them, prisoners. We were all beneath them and they didn't often let us forget that.

Without warning, the door creaked open and a shadowed head peeked inside. "Mellie?" the head whispered.

"Yeah." I was up in an instant and over to the door just as quickly.

"Follow me," he ordered, his nerves obviously on high alert. He was a young man, from what I could see. The shadows were too thick to see much of his face. "Don't talk."

Obediently, I stayed behind him as we hurried through the empty hallways. These steps were familiar to me, but it was different at night. My heart beat wildly in my chest, keeping pace with my light steps. At every turn, I fully expected a guard or Nurse Kaydee to pop out at us and drag me back to my room.

There was no way we were getting away with this. No way.

"We're here," he declared, stopping outside a small metal door with a thin slit that opened up on the bottom. It was probably to give food to her. My stomach lurched.

"Beth is in there?"

"I'll be back to get you in two hours," he whispered, holding up two fingers.

"Two hours?"

"Right before the nurses start their checks, that'll be the best time to get you back to your room without being seen," he explained in a rush. He didn't wait for a response; he opened the metal door and pushed me inside it. The door clicked shut and I heard the lock slide into place.

"WHO'S THERE?" A SMALL voice asked from the darkness.

There wasn't much light in the room, even less in here than there was in my room – I still recognized her voice though. "Beth?"

"Mellie," she breathed out excitedly. "Is that really you?"

"Beth, it's me," I almost cried with my relief. That small voice of excitement was worth every strand of hair I had paid Janice.

"How did you get in here?"

The room was very tiny so it wasn't hard to find her. Dropping to my knees next to her, I took her hand in mine. "Are you ok?" was all I could think of to say.

"No." She brought her shaking hand to my face. "It's so good to see you though, I didn't think I'd ever see you again, Mellie," her voice broke.

Now that I was close enough to see her properly, my heart broke and felt funny in my chest. She was thin and pale, even more pale than usual. Her hair hung in dissaray down her dirty face.

"Don't they feed you in here?" I croaked, pushing her hair back behind her ears. "You look so skinny."

"The food here tastes horrible," she grinned weakly, making the cracks in her lips even more noticeable.

"I think they're going to let you out of here soon," I lied, desperate to make her feel better.

"No they aren't," she sighed. "They won't let me out of this room."

"You didn't kill her, right Beth?" I sucked in a quick breath and held it inside my burning lungs.

"I had to do it."

Her words seemed too large for the solitary room; I couldn't breathe with them in there with us. "Why?"

"Because Leslie was right."

My heart faltered. "What did you say?"

"Leslie told me I had to kill her, and she was right."

"No," I gripped tighter to Beth's hand, "she wasn't right. You never have to kill someone."

"She told me..."

"You never should have listened to Leslie," I gasped, desperation making my voice pinched. "She shouldn't have talked to you."

"It's ok, Mellie," Beth cooed, "she was trying to help me."

"No." My eyes were unable to hold in my tears.

"We probably don't have much time, don't spend it crying."

"You shouldn't have listened to Leslie," I cried.

"I'm so glad I met you," she smiled, wiping away my tears. "I've never liked anyone as much as I like you."

"They have to let you out of here soon. They will, right?"

Beth smiled – the same smile I had been missing for weeks. Unable to help myself, I leaned forward to press my lips to hers.

I WATCHED THE SHADOWS dance on the ceiling in my room. It had been hard to leave Beth in that dirty room, not knowing when or if I would see her again.

Dr Matthews could decide any day to send her to a different place – a prison that was more strict. She would never last in a place like that. My stomach clenched with helplessness.

My chin quivered with the enormous effort it took not to let my tears fall. Beth had told me a long time ago not to cry in here, she didn't want me to let them win. This felt different though.

Beth really did kill the nurse; I had been holding onto the belief that she would never do something so violent. I didn't realize just how tight I was holding onto that notion until it was ripped away from me. Still, I didn't blame Beth.

Leslie told her to kill – this was Leslie's fault.

I never wanted her to talk to Beth – not that I thought she would encourage her to kill someone, but because I didn't want things to be weird. This was worse than weird.

Alone in my room, I had no choice but to face the truth. Leslie was me. Beth had listened to her because she wore my face. This was actually all my fault. That wasn't an easy thing to handle. My sobs came from somewhere deep inside me as I realized another truth – I couldn't trust myself.

"YOU BETTER EAT BEFORE they yell at you," Leslie warned with a wide grin.

"I don't want to eat," I growled, pushing the oatmeal away.

"You knew she did it," her voice changed subtly, despite the fixed grin. "I don't know why you're so upset now."

"Oh really?" My lips trembled as my anger intensified. "You can't figure out why I'm upset?"

"I know she's your friend..."

"You know that she's more than just my friend." I slammed my hand against the cheap metal table, the sound echoed throughout the room.

"Settle down," Leslie ordered through her clenched teeth.

"I can't."

"They're gonna throw you in the hole," she hissed, "and it won't be the same one that they threw Beth in to."

"Don't even say her name." I sucked in my lips, not trusting myself to say anything else. How dare Leslie tease me about Beth after she was the one that got Beth locked away? Leslie needed to listen to what I said, I was the one in charge. All I had to do was tell Dr. Matthews that I was ready for her to go away and she'd be gone.

"What's going on over here?" Nurse Kaydee asked, hoovering over me.

"I don't want to eat."

"Too bad," she huffed, pulling my bowl back to me. "This isn't a restaurant."

"Dr. Matthews said I don't have to eat if I don't want to," I snarled, pushing the bowl back away.

Nurse Kaydee narrowed her eyes. "Are we going to do this again?" she asked in a low voice.

"I don't know," I glared up at her, "do you plan to pull that bowl back?"

Leslie's grin turned to a full chuckle. "I love this nurse," she laughed.

Nurse Kaydee's nostrils flared. "Get to the day room," she ordered. "This is going in your report."

"I don't care about your report." I stood up roughly. "You better put this in there too." With one hand, I shoved the full bowl of oatmeal to the floor. I heard Nurse Kaydee groan as I stormed from the cafeteria.

LESLIE SAT IN OUR USUAL spot at the table closest to the window. I was still fuming though, and not about to sit with her. Spotting Janice, I made a beeline for her table.

"Go away," she huffed without looking up at me.

"You can't tell me where to sit," I growled back. "And I want to sit right here."

"Why?"

"Don't know," I shrugged.

"We're not friends now just because I helped you. That was a business deal."

"What did you have to do anyways?"

Her hand hesitated on the cards. "What are you talking about?"

"How did you get that guy to help me?"

"Don't ask me stupid questions," she snapped.

"It's not a stupid question," I muttered. From the corner of my eye, I watched Leslie move slowly around the room. What was she doing?

"Believe me," she said slowly, "you don't want to know."

There was something in her voice that drew my attention back to her face. What was so important about a bag full of hair that she would do something horrible to get it? How far would I have gone to see Beth? Probably not as far as Janice would go to get what she wanted, I realized with a snarl of disgust.

"Why did you want my hair?"

"You don't want to know that either," she grinned.

"HOW LONG ARE YOU GOING to give me the silent treatment?" Leslie asked, peeling the pillow off my head so I was forced to look up at her.

"I don't have anything to say to you," I declared loudly.

"You haven't had anything to say to me since you saw Beth."

"So?"

"So," she drawled, "you can't ignore me forever."

"I can if I want to," I sulked.

"Why are you so mad at me? I didn't do anything."

"You should have never talked to her."

"Beth?" One eyebrow cocked on her forehead.

"Yeah," I snapped, sucking my lips back into my mouth quickly.

"Beth wanted to talk to me, she asked for me."

"No she didn't," my face darkened as my eyebrows lowered on my head.

"You weren't there, Mellie," she purred. "You don't know what we talked about."

"That's my point." The words burst out of me, unable to stay inside. "I already told you not to talk to Beth. She's my friend, not yours."

"There's one thing that you're going to have to come to terms with sweetie," she sat in her spot by the wall, "what's yours – is also mine."

"Dr. Matthews can you make you go away." We both knew it was an empty threat, but the words were still out there hanging heavily between us.

I PULLED ON MY FINGER ruthlessly, taking a strange delight in the sound of my knuckle popping. Dr. Matthews tapped the end of his pen on the notebook, watching me without saying much.

"I don't know what you want me to say," I finally exploded, shifting slightly on the couch. "I'm upset, of course, but there isn't anything I can do." As mad as I was at Leslie, I couldn't tell him that she had been the one to tell Beth to kill the nurse. It would open up too many questions that I didn't have answers to yet. I had to deal with this on my own.

"I just want you to tell me what you're feeling."

"You always want to know what I'm feeling."

His lips twitched. "That's my job here."

"I don't want to talk about it."

"Then what do you want to talk about?"

"Do we have to talk at all?"

"No." He folded his hands on his lap. "We can just sit here if that's what you prefer."

"Can I just go to my room now? I'm *feeling* tired."

"We have to stay here for the entire hour." He glanced at the clock on the wall. "And we still have thirty seven minutes."

"Are you going to stare at me for thirty seven minutes?"

"It's up to you what we do for the remainder of the time."

Sucking in all the air I could, I let it fill up my cheeks and held it there for as long as possible. Looking up at the clock, it was disheartening to see that only two minutes had passed. "Have you talked to Beth?"

"You already know I can't discuss Beth with you," he nodded slightly.

"You can't even tell me if you talked to her?" I was getting really tired of being the only one forced to talk in these meetings.

"No, I can't."

"She's the only thing I want to talk about," I shrugged.

"Why do you like Beth so much?"

"What kind of question is that?" My lip automatically snarled upwards, already prepared to defend our relationship.

"What is it you find appealing about Beth?"

"She's...soft." That probably wasn't the right word but it was already out there now.

"Physically soft?"

"Just...everything." I kept my eyes on the couch I was sitting on. "Her voice and her smile. You know."

"You thought of her like a friend?"

"Yeah." I swallowed the lump in my throat. "Is there something wrong with making friends?"

"In normal life, making friends would be a healthy thing to do. But this isn't normal."

"You're talking about the hospital?"

"I am."

"Why do you work here if you hate it so much?"

"Right now," he smiled, "I'm here to save you."

THE FLOOR WAS DIRTY but it didn't bother me as much as it should have. I didn't even flinch at the spider that crawled over my foot.

"Are you looking for her too?" I asked the spider in a voice that barely carried past my dry lips. "She's not here."

The deserted hallway was different without Beth there with me, but it was still my favorite place to be. No one was loud here, no one was telling me what to feel. It was ok to cry here.

I took a deep breath and tried to hold it inside, hoping the air would give me some kind of strength. My lungs were tattered though and refused to cooperate; the breath came out in a rush that my mother would have called a sigh.

It wasn't a sigh though, it was grief. I missed my friend, I missed Beth. Was she ok in that dirty room? Was she eating? She looked so thin when I saw her and her eyes were so dark. She wasn't ok and I knew it. And the worst part was that I didn't know when she was going to get out of that room.

Lips trembling hard, I sucked them into my mouth to stop the sobs from coming out of them. Beth told me before that noises echoed back here so we had to be quiet. I pressed my hand tight over mouth and let the tears slide slowly over my fingers.

"WHAT'S GOING ON HERE?" Nurse Kaydee towered over me, her lips pursed so tightly, I suspected they must hurt.

My crossed arms resting heavily on the table in front of me, I scowled back at her. "Nothing," I sneered.

"Eat your lunch," she pointed at the untouched lunch tray that I had pushed away.

"I'm not hungry."

"Mellie."

"I'm not going to eat."

"We're not doing this." She pulled the tray angrily back until it smashed into my arm. "You're eating all this food before you leave this room."

I smiled sweetly. "Guess I'll be here for a while then."

"Mellie."

"Nurse Kaydee."

My eyes stung, the grit was building up in the corners of my eyes. It made them hard to close. It had been a hard few days, my stomach felt funny when I walked. There was no way I was eating anything. And we both knew that Nurse Kaydee couldn't force me to.

"Eat."

"No."

"Is there a problem here?" One of the guards came over to my table. Apparently, our argument was louder than I realized.

"I'm trying to get her to eat," Nurse Kaydee pursed her lips angrily – whether she was mad at me or the guard, I couldn't tell.

"If she doesn't want to eat," he shrugged, "why make her? Who cares if she eats?"

"Thank you," I grinned wide at the man. He wasn't looking to make me happy though.

"Don't smile at me," he snapped.

"We sometimes have to force the patients to eat," she explained to him.

"Prisoners," he corrected.

"They aren't in their right minds," she continued to argue through her clenched jaw, "and we can't let them starve themselves."

"And this one is giving you trouble?"

I didn't like how he called me *this one*.

"This one always gives me trouble."

"You can't force me to eat," I declared harshly.

The guard closed his big hand around the back of my neck and pushed my head down to the table. "You'll do what you're told."

"Not even if you put the food in my mouth yourself," I told him as loudly as possible from the position I was in.

"What did you say to me?" He pulled me back up so I was forced to look up at him.

"I said I'm not eating," I laughed. "Not one single bite."

"You'll do as you're told, prisoner."

"No I won't, guard," I giggled up at him, enraging him further still.

"Do you want to go back to your room?"

"Obviously," I snarled. "That's what I've been saying."

"Then eat," Nurse Kaydee fired. "You can go to your room after lunch."

"I'm not eating." I would have pushed my tray off the table but the guard was still holding me, making it hard to move. "I'm not hungry. Let me go."

"You," his grip tightened briefly on my neck, "don't get to tell me what to do. That's not how this works."

"Get off of me," I screeched, pumping volume into my voice suddenly enough to make him hesitate. It was all I needed – I flung my head backwards as hard as I could and slammed it into his stomach. He jumped backwards as I jumped up off the seat. In the same swift motion, I flung my arm across the table and sent the full tray clashing to the floor.

"Oh my..." Nurse Kaydee swore softly.

"There," I panted. "food is gone." I tuned to look at the shocked guard. "Can I go back to my room now?"

"THAT WAS QUITE A SHOW yesterday," Janice grinned wide at me from across the table.

Leslie hated Janice so I found myself sitting with her more often lately. Maybe it was to keep her away from me or maybe it was just to make her mad. It was working for either one.

"It wasn't a show," I scowled, "I just didn't want their stupid lunch."

"It wasn't that bad," she shrugged.

"Glad you enjoyed your lunch *Janice*."

She giggled as she slid her checker pieces across a board in her one sided game. "I'm starting to like you," she wagged her finger at me.

"Not interested."

Janice laughed again. "I'll always have a piece of you though," she wriggled her eyebrows dramatically.

"You don't have any of me," I snapped.

"Oh but I do." She leaned across the table and ran two fingers lightly against my jagged locks of hair that were sticking up along my scalp.

"You are so weird." I slapped her hand away from me.

"Takes one to know one," she sing songed.

"Whatever," I rolled my eyes.

Across the room, Leslie had taken her usual spot in front of the window. Her arms were crossed tightly over her chest and she was glaring at me. It was impossible to keep my eyes from straying to her. Leslie's anger was a terrible and beautiful thing.

"Who do you keep looking at?" Janice asked loudly, forcing my attention back to her.

"Leslie."

"Your imaginary friend?"

Glaring at her, I refused to comment. It didn't bother me very much when people made fun of me for seeing Leslie – but my temper was shorter than usual lately.

"What does she look like?"

"What?" No one had ever asked me that before.

"Does she look like you?"

"She's prettier than me."

"You're very pretty though."

"Shut up, *Janice.*" Why did she always have to make fun of me?

"What color is her hair?" she continued to probe.

"Kinda black."

"Long?"

"Why are you obsessed with hair?" I snarled.

Janice shrugged. "Why do you see someone who isn't here?"

MY STOMACH HURT. EVEN though I had been starving, I barely ate anything at supper and now I was paying for that. If my stomach kept growling like it was, I'd be forced to eat a nasty breakfast.

"You don't have to eat," Leslie argued with my silent musings.

"I will if I want to."

"Humans can go three days without eating." She held up three fingers in the dimly lit room.

"Why would I want to go three days without eating?"

"To prove a point."

"Which is?" I rolled over so I could see her better.

"Which is," she raised both eyebrows dramatically, "that you don't have to eat their food if you don't want to."

"They already know that I don't have to." I had pushed the food on to the floor, wasn't that a pretty clear statement?

"Prove it."

My stomach rumbled loudly in the empty room. "By not eating for three days?"

"That's one way," she shrugged.

I rolled away from her smug smile, holding tightly to my stomach. I was so hungry that even the oatmeal sounded good, but maybe Leslie was right.

"You know I'm right," came her whisper behind me.

"Maybe," I sulked. "I mean, they really can't force me to eat."

"They force you to do everything else."

"Yeah."

"But that's the one thing that they have no control over."

"I guess you're right."

"Of course I'm right." I heard the smugness in her voice.

"I'M NOT MOVING," I declared again in a huffy voice.

"You already know that's my seat, Mellie," Carrie shrilled.

"I don't see your name on it."

I was exhausted, beyond tired. As soon as I came into the day room, I sank into the first available seat. Now skinny Carrie was trying to take it from me. Tired as I was, she wasn't getting my seat.

"Get up," she squealed like a stupid pig.

"No." Keeping my head down, I refused to look up at her. "This is my seat now."

"If you want your eyeballs to stay in your head, you better move," she growled, leaning down to try and force me to look up.

My laughter bubbled up quietly from my tight chest. "You think you're big enough to make me?" I chuckled, finally looking up at her.

"Yeah, I do." She swung her arm out to smack me, but I ducked out of her way in time and she only got the empty air.

"Keep your hands off of me," my laughter died quickly – replaced by an anger that I could hardly contain.

"Hit her," Leslie snarled. "She deserves it; she was gonna hit you. Self defense."

Carrie was standing too close for me to get up so I just flung both hands out and pushed hard against her legs. She stumbled backwards enough for me to jump up.

"Back off," I growled when she made another wild attempt to swing at me. "I'm not playing."

"I'm not afraid of you," she sneered. "Stay out of my seat."

"You think every seat is yours." I swatted her hands away from my face.

"I really like your haircut," she taunted. "Did you get it done at shears?"

"You're so funny, Carrie," I laughed again, swaying slightly on my feet. "Did you think of that all by yourself?"

"Do you see anyone else here?" She threw her arms wide.

There were other people though, I didn't know what she meant. I couldn't focus on any of the faces. The entire room was spinning, I couldn't see anything.

The next thing I knew, Carrie's face was gone too and I was staring up at the ceiling. Voices exploded all around me but they were coming from far away, almost as if I were under the water. It was impossible to know if they were trying to pull me out or if they were holding me under.

"Get back everyone," came one clear voice. The bright pink shirt must have belonged to a nurse.

"Can you hear me, Mellie?" the nurse yelled into my face.

Of course I could hear her, she was screaming in my face. My voice wasn't coming out loud enough for her to hear me, hopefully she would see my eyes rolling.

"She's passing out," she said to someone I couldn't see. "Get everyone out of here."

"We need to get an IV started," the other nurse declared. "She hasn't been eating."

"Clear the room," she insisted, "and get me an IV bag. Her pulse is too low."

"Let's get her back to her room."

"Mellie, can you hear me? Open your eyes," she called loudly. I felt her fingers tap lightly against my cheeks.

"Don't take that IV," a new voice hissed in my ear.

"What?" I turned weakly to the voice that was most familiar to me.

Leslie watched the nurses working. "They're gonna try to make you take that IV."

It was a struggle to move my head enough to see the IV bag. "What are you doing?" I asked weakly. "I don't want that."

"Just lay still," Nurse Kaydee cooed. "You're fine."

"I don't want that." I pushed her hand away from my arm where she was rubbing it with a cotton ball.

"Don't move," she said again, as if she hadn't heard me say anything at all.

"She's going to put the IV in," Leslie warned me. "It's their way of forcing you to eat. You can't let them do it."

"Stop," I panted. "Don't stick me with any needles."

"It won't hurt," she patted me roughly. "We're trying to help you."

"I don't want your help." I wanted to kick my feet, I wanted to slap the nurses away from me, I wanted to jump to my feet and run from the room. But I couldn't move.

Leslie's face blurred around the edges. "Mellie," she whispered just before everything went black.

"ARE YOU FEELING ANY better, Mellie?" Dr. Matthews asked, his fingers laced together under his chin.

"Better than what?" I snapped out, then pursed my lips tightly.

"You passed out in the day room."

"Because of that crack head, Carrie." Why did everything always turn into what I did wrong?

"Because you haven't been eating," he corrected.

"Humans can live for days without food," I informed him, knowing full well I sounded like a child arguing with a parent.

"Three weeks," he nodded.

"Really?" Leslie said it was only three days.

"But it doesn't take that long to pass out."

"I didn't pass out," I argued, "I just fell down."

"You had to be carried to your room," he gently reminded me.

"I was feeling dizzy," I muttered, "but it was because of Carrie. She tried to attack me."

"Was Leslie there?"

"Yes."

"What did she say?"

"She told me not to let the nurses give me the IV," I recalled hazily.

His stoically calm face reacted slightly, confusion and a bit of anger chased each other briefly through his eyebrows. "Leslie doesn't want you to eat," he concluded.

"She doesn't want me to be controlled," I corrected.

"Explain what you mean." He took his pen back in his hand.

"The nurses can't force me to eat," I echoed Leslie's words to me.

"Not eating is making you physically weak."

"Can't force me." The words jerked out, as if they were the only things I had to hold on to.

Dr. Matthews visibly sighed his frustration. "If it becomes a bigger issue with your health, you will force me to give the orders to tube feed you."

"You can't."

"I will."

Tears sprang to my already burning eyes and my lip started shaking like I was two years old. "Why is this happening to me, Dr. Matthews?"

"You need to eat," he said quietly, "you'll feel a lot better if you stop listening to Leslie."

"WHAT DID HE SAY?" LESLIE whispered.

My head rolled to one side so I could see her sitting on the floor. "Same thing he says every day," I murmured, my lips barely moving.

"He said that fight was your fault?"

"Yep."

The nurses were continuing to give me an IV of some clear stuff every day but I still refused to eat. Dr. Matthews hadn't made good on his threat to tube feed me yet, it was probably just a matter of time now. I could feel that I was weak, even getting out of bed was a struggle.

"Is he mad that you aren't eating?"

"Yep."

Leslie smiled wide. "Good. Let him be mad, how does he think you feel?"

I couldn't tell how I felt anymore. Things were really getting hazy these days. "I don't care if he's mad," I sighed deeply.

"Of course you don't care." Her eyebrows puckered up. "He's an idiot and they can't tell you what to do."

"I just want Beth to come back." Tears fell from my eyes and slid over my nose to fall on the uncomfortable pillow.

"It won't be long now, you just have to stay strong."

"I don't like this place, Leslie."

"You just had a hard day," she comforted me. "Tomorrow will be better."

"I hope so," I croaked.

A bright light flared to life as the door was flung open. "What's going on here?" Nurse Kaydee demanded.

"Nothing."

"Who are you talking to?"

I hesitated only slightly. "Leslie."

Nurse Kaydee looked around the empty room and nodded. "How are you feeling?"

"Fine," I shrugged awkwardly from my place on the bed.

"Does your stomach still hurt?"

"I guess so."

"Why don't you want to eat, Mellie?"she asked, abruptly dropping her bristly demeanor.

"I don't like the food here."

"That's not the reason." Leaving the door propped open, she sat down on the edge of my bed. "The food is bad, but not bad enough to starve yourself."

"I'm just...tired."

"Does Leslie tell you not to eat?"

"She just doesn't want you to tell me what to do." My lips cracked, they had the tangy taste of blood. "She said you control everything else, but not this."

"We're trying to help you, kiddo."

"Leslie is helping me."

"Leslie is making you starve yourself."

"No," I shook my head weakly. "Leslie is the only person in this whole world that cares about me." I couldn't stop more tears from falling.

"When she tells you that," Nurse Kaydee said thickly, "you can know for absolute certainty that it is a lie."

"What?"

"That's a lie because I care about you, kiddo."

"YOU KNOW," LESLIE SAT on the bench across from me and watched me shovel oatmeal into my mouth, "I think it's borderline sexual abuse."

"What is?" I choked around a full mouth.

"Nurse Kaydee," she sneered, "and her whole *I care about you* speech."

"She was just being nice," I scowled back after I had swallowed my too large bite.

Leslie regarded me with narrowed eyes. "I still don't know why you couldn't hold out on the eating thing."

"I was hungry." I shoved half a piece of bread in my mouth. "You're weak."

Maybe she was right but I couldn't see how making myself too weak to walk was a good idea. I couldn't help Beth at all if I couldn't get out of bed.

"The food isn't really that bad."

"That isn't the point and you know it." She puffed the air into her cheeks and blew it out angrily.

"Hurry up, Parker," Nurse Kaydee snapped as she passed. "Eat so you can go see Dr. Matthews."

"Almost done," I grinned, popping the rest of my bread into my mouth.

"I don't know what you're so happy about," she sneered. "It's just bread."

"With butter," I defended the almost stale bread with butter smashed into the middle.

"She has a crush on you," Leslie insisted. "It's gross."

"She's too old to have a crush on me," I frowned at her. "She's just being nice."

"Wake up, Mellie," Leslie barked, "no one here is nice unless they want something from you. Just ask Janice."

The bread in my mouth became a little harder to swallow. I knew that wasn't what Nurse Kaydee was thinking but still... Why did Leslie have to say things like that?

"I'M NOT TALKING TO you right now," I hissed behind me to Leslie. "So you can stop following me."

"It's not like I have anything better to do," she snarled. "No one else can see me."

"I know," I growled, "but I'm not going to talk to you."

"I see that."

"Into the day room, Parker," Nurse Kaydee ordered brashly. "The hallway is not a place to socialize."

"I'm just telling Leslie to stop following me," I tried to explain.

"I love when she looks at you like that," Leslie chuckled.

"Like what?"

"Like you're a complete nutcase."

"No she isn't." My eyes narrowed as I studied Nurse Kaydee.

"Is there a problem, Parker?" she asked, squaring her impressive shoulders.

"No," I grumbled through a clenched jaw.

"Then get your butt into the day room." She pointed to the open double doors.

"It's like she's obsessed with your butt," Leslie scowled.

"Shut up."

"What did you just say?" Nurse Kaydee glared down at me.

"I wasn't talking to you."

"Go."

Leslie laughed behind me as I entered the full day room. "You almost got me in trouble," I informed her with a furrowed brow.

"Whatever," she puffed out her lips. "Nurse Kaydee *cares* about you. Remember?"

"I'm going to sit with Janice." I couldn't help but smile at the clear distaste on her face.

"Why are you besties with her all of a sudden?"

"I owe her a lot."

"You owe who a lot?" Carrie asked loudly, pushing roughly past me to take one of the spots on the long couch.

"None of your business." I still didn't forgive her for trying to fight with me before.

Carrie pulled her boney knees up to her chest and continued to glare at me. "You're so crazy," she made her eyes go wide.

"All the best people are crazy," Leslie sing – songed on her way to the window seat.

"Can I play?" I asked Janice, sitting across from her at a small table.

"No."

"Why not?"

"I don't want to play with you."

"I'm a fun person," I insisted, making a grab for the cards on the table.

"I don't like crazy people."

"Oh," I laughed loudly, "that's the only kind of people that live here."

"What's the matter with you?" She stopped shuffling her cards to stare at me. "This isn't band camp, we're not here to make friends."

"So?" I shrugged wildly.

"I'm serious, what's wrong with you?"

"I'm mad at Leslie," I blurted. "I don't want to talk to her."

"I thought she was your friend."

"I think that she's..." My tongue darted across my bottom lip.

"She's what?"

"I think she's trying to make me crazy."

Janice blinked slowly. "I have no idea if I'm supposed to laugh or feel sorry for you."

"YOU CAN'T JUST IGNORE me, Mellie," Leslie yelled close to my ear.

I ducked my head quickly away from her, pressing my ear against my shoulder without being obvious. The nurses had us lined up in the hall to get our pills from them as if they were the ice cream truck handing out treats to the neighborhood children.

Leslie, clearly, was getting tired of my silent treatment.

"Hey!"

Wincing away from her scream, I had to twirl away to the other side. I had already decided, if I just stopped talking to Leslie then she would go away. And I really needed her to go away; she was making it hard to think straight.

"I'm not just going to go away," she snarled.

I pressed as close as I could get to the girl in front of me. "Stop touching me," the girl growled, pushing me backwards.

"See what happens when you ignore me," Leslie threw her arm at the still scowling girl.

"Leave me alone," I hissed from the side of my mouth.

"I won't leave you alone," Leslie snarled. "What makes you think I would leave you alone? I promised I wouldn't."

"Parker," the nurse called out my name, shaking a small white cup of pills towards me. "Meds."

"What?" My head snapped at the sound of my name but it was hard to concentrate on her.

"Take your pills, Parker," the nurse repeated, anger coloring her voice.

"I will." My hand snapped out in an automatic gesture to accept my cure.

"Don't you swallow those pills," Leslie screamed, trying to shove the cup out of my hands.

"Stop it," I scowled, pushing her hand back away. "I want to take these."

"Why would you want to?" she spat.

"So that you'll go away." I tried to move my lips as little as possible but the nurse was still watching me with her narrowed eyes.

"Just..." Nurse Kaydee shook her head and let her eyes close the rest of the way, but only briefly. "Just swallow the pills, Parker. You can talk to Leslie when you get back to your room."

Leslie's small laugh is what set me over the edge. Not that it would have taken much.

"Shut up!" I screamed, whirling on her as she moved back in front of me.

"Excuse me?" I heard Nurse Kaydee ask from far away.

Leslie laughed again. "Why would I want to shut up?" Her face contorted with rage.

"Because I told you too," I snapped back at her, my words ripping the anger from her face. Shock and sadness took its place, momentarily making me drop my guard.

"I'm only trying to help you, Mellie," she said in a small voice. "All I've ever wanted to do was help you."

"Like you helped Beth?" I snarled.

Leslie's eyes narrowed. "What happened to her is not my fault," she growled through thin lips.

"You told her to kill that..."

"Stop talking," she yelled out, cutting off the accusation. "Don't say anything else while people are watching us you stupid girl."

Glancing around, I realized just how right she was. Everyone in the hall was staring directly at me.

"SHE WON'T TALK TO ME," Leslie told Dr. Matthews, waving her arm angrily in my direction.

His eyes narrowed as they moved slowly over my face. "Why are the two of you not speaking?" he asked carefully.

"She blames me for what happened to her nut job girlfriend," Leslie snapped out before I could reply. Her glare darkened as she settled back against the couch.

"I would like to talk to Mellie on her own." Dr. Matthews tapped his notebook with one long finger.

"Too bad," Leslie snarled. "I'm not going anywhere until she agrees to talk to me."

"I'm never talking to her again," I replied angrily, making sure to only look at Dr. Matthews.

"You can't ignore me forever, Mellie."

"So you keep saying, Leslie."

"Thought you weren't talking to me." Her eyes went wide.

"That doesn't count as talking to you," I sneered. "Stop trying to make me."

"Mellie." Dr. Matthews called my name, forcing my attention back to him. "If you truly don't want to see Leslie anymore, there are things we can do to help you."

"What sort of things?" Leslie asked sharply.

"Mellie?" Dr. Matthews' eyebrows furrowed deeply.

"What sort of things?" I echoed Leslie.

"We can try different medications. If you really don't want to see Leslie anymore, the pills will help."

"I already swallow your pills," I pointed out with a scrunched nose.

"There are many kinds of medication that will help you, Mellie. We just have to find the right combination."

"Do you really think they would work?" I moved my eyes sideways to take in Leslie.

"They will if you want them to."

"I do," I said softly, not looking at him. Leslie's anger was fading and I didn't like what was replacing it.

"HEY," LESLIE SNAPPED her fingers in front of my face. "Did you hear me?"

"What?" Blinking rapidly, I refocused on her. "I hear you." It had been weeks since Dr. Matthews put me on a new diet of meds and it had made no difference. Leslie still sat across from me in the day room, glaring at Nurse Kaydee.

"Then what did I say?" she demanded.

"You were talking about the nurse."

"Oh," Leslie held up her hands in a dramatic flare. "So now she's *the* nurse."

"She's always been the nurse," I shrugged. "What do you have against her anyways?"

"She's creepy."

"No she isn't. She's nice to me."

Her eyes went wide, comically wide. "Nice to you? Are you kidding me?"

Why did my face feel so hot? "I know what you're trying to insinuate," I hissed, "and I'm not going to let you do that."

"I am only looking out for you Mellie." She grasped her hands to her chest, still being dramatic.

"Stop it."

"Med pass," Nurse Kaydee called out, suddenly looming over my table with her small cup of pills.

"Oh," I breathed out, stretching my hand to accept the pills. "You came at just the right time." I pointed my glare back across the table.

"Is Leslie still bothering you?"

"Dr. Matthews said these pills would make her go away."

Leslie rolled her eyes. "I'm not going anywhere. Not ever."

"Nothing is a magical cure," Nurse Kaydee smiled, making Leslie grunt her disapproval. "It just takes time."

"She is so flirting with you," Leslie hissed. "Waiting for you to get out of here so she can really make her move. Gross!"

With my own flare of dramatics, I flung the small pills into my mouth and swallowed them loudly.

SITTING UPRIGHT IN my bed with my knees pulled tightly to my chest, I glared at Leslie. My eye was twitching rapidly, my foot was shaking; and still, she wouldn't stop talking. She was trying to drive me crazy, I knew she was. And it was working.

"What's wrong, Mellie," she smiled sweetly, "can't sleep?"

"Three days," I growled, holding up three shaking fingers. "You haven't let me sleep for three days."

"That's because you hurt my feelings." Although she still smiled, her eyes narrowed and turned cold.

"You're not real, how can you have feelings?"

That was enough to wipe the stupid smile off her face. "If you keep saying things like that, I'm not going to let you talk to Dr. Matthews anymore."

"You can't tell me what I can or can't do."

"Can't I?" One eyebrow shot up on her smooth forehead.

A chill ran up my arm but I ignored it. "Pretty soon you won't even be here."

"I already told you," her voice exploded, "I'm not leaving."

"I'm not letting you hurt anyone else, Leslie."

"Ethan deserved what he got."

"And Beth?"

"I helped Beth."

"You got her locked up."

"She's been locked up for a very long time," Leslie replied softly. "I helped her."

"Will you please just let me sleep, Leslie?" There was no point in arguing about Beth in the middle of the night. It was only going to make me feel worse.

"When you agree to stop taking those pills."

"I can't," I croaked. Eyes stinging, I stared hard at her, willing her to understand without words. She always understood me without any explanations. Why couldn't she see that I was afraid of her, scared of what she was making me do?

"Then I'm not leaving," she said calmly.

"Fine." Balling my hands into fists, I rubbed my tears roughly away and scooted off the bed. "If you won't leave so I can sleep, I'll make you leave."

"And how do you plan to do that?"

"Hey!" I screamed out loud, not at Leslie.

The nurses were out in the hallways all through the night, paroling to make sure there was no trouble. And if they heard even a trace of it, they would act fast. Especially after what happened to Nurse Lee.

"Hey," I screamed again, this time pounding on the solid metal door with my balled fist. "Let me out of here."

It didn't take me long to get what I wanted.

"What is all this noise?" a pale faced woman asked, creaking the door open just enough to stick her head inside. "What do you want, Parker?"

"I want out of here."

I heard her tongue click against the roof of her mouth in an impatient gesture. "That isn't going to happen."

"I want out of this room," I repeated, louder this time.

"Go back to bed." She moved so she could square her impressive shoulders at me, letting the door swing open further.

"I'm not sleeping in this room with *her.*" Leslie had moved to stand close to my side.

"There's no one in here except you."

"Leslie is here and I'm not staying in here with her." I lunged suddenly past the surprised nurse and managed to make it out into the hallway before she could grab a hold of me.

"Parker," she grunted. "Don't make this harder on everyone. Just stay where you're supposed to stay."

"I won't!" Flailing my arms as wildly as possible, I made contact with the side of her head - earning myself more grunts.

"Hold still."

"Leave me alone." I squirmed harder until her grip loosened enough to allow me to kick her.

"Assistance," she screamed down the empty hall. "Assistance!"

A guard and another nurse were there almost immediately, holding me down for her while she ran to get a needle. I knew this needle – this was what I had wanted. Now I would sleep even with Leslie there.

I glanced over at her, planning to laugh in her face, but Leslie was smiling already. She grinned wide down at me while they pumped the tranquilizers into my arm.

"Why are you laughing?" I panted up at her. I didn't hear her response.

THE FORGOTTEN HALLWAY was darker than usual; I hadn't been able to sneak in after lunch so I waited until dinner time. The shadows were deeper now, the draft was colder. I didn't care though – at least it was quiet.

I sank to the floor, suddenly more tired than I had been in a long time.

My thoughts, as they so often did when the rest of the world was silent, went to Beth. She was probably thinking of me too, I realized with a small sniff. She had once told me that the person you thought of the most often was more than likely also thinking of you. It was sweet at the time, but now it only made me sad.

The tears started out slow, in just the corners of my eyes. Once full, they spilled over onto my cheeks and dripped off my chin. It wouldn't be long now and I'd be full out sobbing; I could feel it building in my trembling chest.

Attempting to hold the sound inside myself, I slapped my hand over my mouth.

"You're not allowed to be back here," came a familiar snarky voice. Leslie had found me.

"I know," I sobbed. "They won't catch me though."

"Well I heard you so I'm pretty sure the entire floor will notice the sound of blubbering sooner or later. This place is supposed to be deserted."

Leslie was the last person I wanted to see right now. Every time I saw her once comforting face, I was angry all over again.

"If I do get caught back here, it will be because I'm talking to you," I growled between sobs.

"So don't talk to me."

"Why can't you just go away."

"You know, the first time you told me that – it kind of hurt my feelings; but after a while, it starts to lose its sting." She leaned casually against the wall and stared down at me. A look of disgust marred her pretty features.

"If you would just listen the first time, I wouldn't have to keep repeating myself."

"I could say the same to you," she smiled without warmth. "It's amazing how alike we are, huh?"

"I don't want to keep talking to you, Leslie."

Her arms fell loosely to her sides. "Why not?"

"Because."

"Because why?"

"I don't have to tell you." I watched a tiny ant crawl across the floor and wondered if I should kill it or let it get away. A chill ran up my spine; of course I would let it get away.

"Tell me or I'm not going anywhere. Is it something Dr. Matthews said to you?"

"It's because...I'm mad at you," I admitted in a low voice, still watching the ant.

"Mad at me?" I didn't have to be looking at her to know how low her eyebrows were resting on her forehead.

"Yeah."

"Why?"

Did I really want to get into this with her? She had to know it was because of Beth, why did I need to say it out loud?

Pressing my lips tight together, I shook my head quickly back and forth.

"Oh, are we going to play this game again?"

"Just forget it."

"You're like a child, Mellie. That's why things like this always happen to you."

Things like this?

"Maybe your life would be different if you learned how to open your mouth and tell people what you're thinking – what you're *really* thinking."

Anger surged through me, throbbing violently in my veins until I was shaking. "You want to know what I'm REALLY thinking?" I seethed. My head snapped up so she could see my face.

"Yes," she seethed back at me.

"You made Beth kill that nurse," I flung at her, my voice getting louder by the second. "You talked her into it because she was getting too close to me."

"Ridiculous," she snorted. "I was helping Beth because she's my friend."

"No she isn't. She's MY friend, not yours."

"Same thing," Leslie shrugged.

"No, it's..."

"It is," she cut me off. "We're the same."

"Not to Beth."

"Do you really think Beth would listen to anything I said?" Leslie pointed one finger into her own chest. In direct contrast to me, she was getting softer as my anger swelled.

Thoughts that I didn't want to have swirled inside my head. Why did she have to be right? What did that mean? "Beth...,"

I croaked her name, "Beth only trusted you because ... to everyone else, you wear my face."

"I personally think you have a fine face, don't know why you changed it."

"What have I done?"

"We helped free her." Leslie moved so she was standing close to me. "You know what it's like to be in a prison that no one else can see, you should be happy for Beth."

"Don't say her name," I hissed.

"Mellie."

"Stay away from me."

"This again?"

"GET AWAY!"

"What is going on back here?" a new voice suddenly invaded the hallway. "What are you doing in here?" Nurse Kaydee asked, her mouth fell open.

"How did you find me?" I sobbed, still shouting.

"You were missing at count," her eyes narrowed, "so I came back to find you and heard the screaming."

"Screaming?" I swiped the tears from my eyes so I could see her better.

"Let's get you back to your room, Mellie."

"I can't let her..."

"Can't let her what?"

"No," I shook my head frantically. "I mean that I can't let myself."

"Ok," she said slowly.

"I can't let myself hurt anyone else, Nurse Kaydee."

LIKE A CHILD, I WANTED to hide my face away from Dr. Matthews, I didn't want him to see me crying. Obviously, he already knew I was – he could hear me. My shoulders shook with my sobs, but I still covered my face.

"You can look at me, Mellie," he soothed. "There's nothing to be afraid of here."

"I know," I gasped through my fingers. "I don't want you to look at me."

"It's my job to look at you," his smile showed through his words.

"You know what I mean."

"Why are you crying? Are you sad?"

Sad? I guess that was one way of putting it. "Yes."

"Can you tell me why?"

Exasperated, I let my hands fall away from my face. "Isn't it obvious?"

"Tell me," he smiled gently.

"I'm hurting people, Dr. Matthews."

He paused in his incessant pen tapping. "Who are you hurting?"

"I hurt Ethan Sturgis...and..."

"And?"

"Beth."

"How did you hurt Beth?"

I hesitated, but it was time to be truthful. "Leslie is the one who told her to kill that nurse."

"Did Leslie tell you that?"

"Beth told me." I leaned all the way forward on the couch. "When I went to see her in that room, she told me she talked to Leslie."

As if trying to get away from me, Dr. Matthews leaned further back in his own seat. "There are a lot of things you don't know about Beth. You realize that I can't tell you any of her details, but neither you nor Leslie made her kill that nurse. Beth is very unwell."

"She was fine until she talked to Leslie."

"She was never fine, Mellie. She was only having some good days – probably because of your friendship."

"Leslie looks like me to other people," I gushed. "Beth trusted her because she looks like me. That's why she killed that nurse."

Dr. Matthews took a deep breath and let it out slowly. "It's true that Leslie is a danger to you and to other people, but you can't blame yourself for what happened to Beth." He pressed his lips together and sighed again. "A difficult life, a chemical unbalance, and no help from the adults in her life are to blame for Beth's illness. She makes her own choices though, just as we all do."

Dr. Matthews was wrong though. We didn't all get to make our own choices. I wanted to tell him that, I wanted to cry and throw myself at his feet to beg for help, I wanted to make him give me the right pills that would make Leslie disappear for good. I couldn't do any of that though – not with Leslie sitting next to me, glaring and puffing out her cheeks.

THE EGGS WERE EVEN worse than the oatmeal. I stuck my fork in the middle of the yellow blob on my plate and it all came up off the plate at once, stuck to my fork like a lollipop of cold scrambled eggs. My top lip snarled up.

"What is this?"

"Just eat, Parker." Nurse Kaydee was less than amused. "This isn't some fancy hotel and you know it."

"Where's the oatmeal?"

"You hate oatmeal." Her lips pressed together to form an angry straight line just below her nose.

"I was getting used to it."

"Hurry up and eat your breakfast."

"You're not eating that," Leslie informed me, her own angry line of lips on her face.

"Why not?"

"Because she doesn't get to be the boss of you," she flung her arm in the direction of Nurse Kaydee, who was now harassing someone else over their breakfast. "I'm tired of her telling you what to do all the time. No wonder she's single."

"You don't know if she's single," I muttered. "And she kind of *is* the boss of me."

"No she isn't, she's just some stupid nurse."

My eyes shifted to Nurse Kaydee. She wasn't as bad as Leslie said she was. Besides for a teacher in eighth grade, she was the only adult who seemed to care what happened to me. To everyone else, I was invisible. I never got good enough grades to matter to anyone and I never got in enough trouble to get noticed. It wasn't terrible that someone would care if I ate or not.

"Hey," Leslie suddenly pounded both of her fists on the table in front of us. "Did you hear what I said?"

"Yes."

"Then?"

"I'm not eating it," I growled.

"Good." She didn't smile.

Even if Leslie wasn't there to tell me what to do, I wouldn't have eaten those eggs. "It's disgusting anyways," I muttered out loud to no one.

I STOOD NEXT TO THE opened glass doors, puffing air in and out of my cheeks. "I wish I could just go back to my room today," I whispered to Leslie. All the tables in the day room were full and I hated sitting on the couch. When someone else sat next to me on the old couch, they always squished way too close into my space.

"Every time you do that, they pump you full of too many of their meds," Leslie complained loudly. "It makes you tired."

Sleeping didn't sound like a bad idea, I silently argued. "Well, I'm not sitting on the couch." I forced my thoughts away from the times Beth and I shared the couch.

"You don't have to." Scanning the room, Leslie twisted her face up into an exaggerated sneer.

"Everywhere else is full." I followed her lead and searched the room myself. "I'll just sit with Janice," I decided. There was only one other girl sitting with Janice and they probably wouldn't complain too loudly if I sat with them.

"No," Leslie snapped.

"Why not?"

"I don't like Janice."

"I don't like her either but there's no where else."

"Make her move." She jutted her chin in the direction of an old lady sitting by herself at a corner table, counting something that was only visible to her. I watched her finger slide the imaginary object across the table and add it to a pile.

"I can't make her move."

"Sure you can."

"I 'm not going to."

"Why?"

"Because."

"Do it."

"She's not hurting anyone there. Let's just leave her alone."

"I want that table," Leslie's voice had started to rise. A few heads turned in our direction.

"Just..."

"Are you going to tell her to move or am I?" One eyebrow cocked high on her forehead, I wasn't going to win this argument.

"I will," I growled through clenched teeth.

Unwillingly, I shuffled over to the corner table and stared down at the woman. "Excuse me?"

"What?" she barked.

"Will you move?"

"Screw you."

"Hey," Leslie pushed past me angrily. "Move your ass, you crazy old bitch!"

"Leslie," I hissed. "I said I was going to ask, remember?"

"You did ask – and she said no."

"Let me handle this." I tried to shove her back but she wouldn't budge.

Suddenly, the lady sprang up from her chair. "You're crazier than I thought," she muttered on her way past me to the couch.

Smiling wide, Leslie flung herself in one of the empty chairs. "That went well," she declared happily.

"Well?" My eyebrows scrunched up. "Now she thinks I'm crazy."

"You are crazy, Mellie."

If she was trying to make me feel better, it didn't work. Huffing slightly, I leaned back in my seat and crossed my arms over my chest. All around me, people were staring and avoiding eye contact at the same time. "Do you think they heard me talking to you?" I asked Leslie.

"I'd say it's a safe bet that they can hear you," Leslie giggled. "Who cares though? Let them stare."

THE SEATS OUTSIDE DR. Matthews' office were hard. I sat there alone, watching the clock tick closer to the hour I was allowed back to see him. Leslie was there too, but she was leaning against the far wall – watching me.

"I've decided something," she announced suddenly.

"What have you decided?" My eyes made a lazy arch to look at her and then back at the clock.

"I don't want you to talk to Dr. Matthews anymore."

"It's not your choice to make," I reminded her. "They make me come and see him almost every single day."

"I'll talk to him instead of you."

My tongue clicked against the roof of my mouth. "I like talking to Dr. Matthews."

"That's the problem."

"Why?"

"You tell him too much."

"He's not allowed to tell anyone."

"I don't think it works like that here," she scoffed. "You're in a prison – he can tell whatever he wants to the police."

"I don't care."

"Well, I do."

"You haven't been wanting me to talk to anyone lately."

"You don't need friends in here; you have me."

I didn't respond or look at her.

"You had a friend and look how that turned out."

A flush started to burn in my cheeks. "And who's fault is that?"

"It doesn't matter," she shook her head firmly from side to side. "I've already decided that you aren't going to talk to Dr. Matthews anymore."

"You can't stop me from talking, Leslie." But her small grin made me wonder if I was right about that.

"HOW HAVE YOU BEEN FEELING, Mellie?" Dr. Matthews asked in his soft way.

"You won't be talking to Mellie today," Leslie interjected before I could say anything.

"Why not?"

"She doesn't want to talk to you anymore."

"That's not true," I squeaked.

Leslie turned slitted eyes in my direction. "I told you not to say anything," she reminded me.

"Why don't you want Mellie to speak to me?" Dr. Matthews asked Leslie. His brow darkened slightly, but he kept his calm voice and face.

"You're a bad influence on her."

"Because I tell her the truth?"

"You tell her *your* truth," Leslie argued, jutting her bottom lip out slightly.

"And what is your truth, Leslie?" His head cocked to one side, as if he were genuinely interested in whats he had to say.

Leslie shifted awkwardly on the couch next to me. "I'm not here to hurt Mellie."

"And yet, here she is, locked away like an animal for a crime that you did."

I winced at Dr. Matthews words. Did he have to be so harsh to Leslie?

"She needs me."

"Why?"

"If I'm not here, she would never stick up for herself. She would just let people walk all over her."

"Like every other person on the planet, Mellie would learn to stick up for herself. She doesn't need anyone else to do it for her."

Pressing her lips together, Leslie shook her head stubbornly. "She needs me," she repeated. "You weren't there, you don't know." She turned to look at me, the depth of her knowledge piercing my resolve.

Leslie was right about some things. No one else understood the things she did. Maybe I did need her. What kind of life would I be living if she hadn't come to help me?

"It's settled," she declared abruptly, looking back at Dr. Matthews, "I'm staying and Mellie isn't going to be talking to you anymore."

Dr. Matthews took a deep breath and let it back out heavily. "Mellie," he took his glasses off and stared at me, "don't let her take over too much of your life. We're going to get you sorted, I promise."

"Hmph," Leslie flung herself back against the couch, arms crossed angrily over her chest.

"WHY ARE WE IN HERE again?" Leslie groaned, slamming her fists against the cold metal of the locked door.

"Because you bit Dr. Matthews," I growled, leaning my head against the wall behind me.

There was no bed in solitary, just a thin mattress on the floor. Not knowing what kind of people or critters had slept on it, I chose not to lay or sit on it. We had been back here for three days though and my bones were starting to feel sore.

"Stop hitting the door," I told Leslie – again.

"I want out of here."

"That isn't helping."

"It's better than what you're doing."

I'm not doing anything."

"Exactly." In a huff, she squatted down in front of me. "Where is your fight?"

"What are we fighting? A metal door?" They weren't going to let me out until they thought I had learned my lesson. Continuing to fight the metal door was a good way to stay locked up.

"I didn't even bite him that hard." She flung herself back on the filthy mattress. "He should have just told me what he was writing in that damn notebook."

"He never says what he's writing," I reminded her dully.

"It was about me, I have a right to know."

"I just hope we get out soon. We're not helping Beth at all from in here."

Leslie huffed again. "They can't keep us in here forever. How long do you think is the longest they can keep us in here?"

"I don't know," I shrugged. "We'll just have to stay here until they open the door."

"This is the problem with you, Mellie," she said, disgusted. "You just lay down and take whatever they do to you."

"Should I just start biting everyone that makes me mad? That seems to be working well for you." I slapped lightly on the hard floor.

Leslie rolled her eyes and got up to pound on the door some more.

I CHEWED WITHOUT TASTING my food. All around the cafeteria there was a buzz of voices but it was difficult to hear a single voice. Only when Nurse Kaydee loomed over me did I turn my face away from the wall.

"Good to see you out of the hole," she grunted.

Although I knew she was teasing, my lips refused to move so I could grin at her like she wanted me too. Nothing on my face seemed to be working right anymore. Maybe I had spent to much time alone with just Leslie for company; everything felt different somehow. My arms felt too heavy, as if they no longer belonged to me.

"You alright?"

"Yeah," Leslie fired up at her. "Just keep on walking."

"I'm fine Nurse Kaydee," I sighed. I was tired of fighting Leslie, tired of telling everyone I was fine, and tired of being in this place. "I'm just tired."

"After lunch you can go ahead and lay down instead of coming to the day room." She smiled kindly before walking away from my table.

"YOU KNOW WHAT I WISH?" I asked quietly, to no one in particular.

"What do you wish for?" Carrie asked, slapping a nine of diamonds on the discard pile in the middle of the table.

"You can't lay a diamond," Janice screeched, flinging the card back at Carrie.

"Oh-ho," Carrie drawled the single syllable out into four. "Did you write the rule book, *Janice*?"

"Maybe you should just go back to your coloring books," she growled across the table.

"I wish I was normal," I said dully while they continued to argue over the rules of the card game.

"Normal," Leslie scowled darkly. "Who the hell wants to be normal?"

"Me."

"You what?" Carrie demanded, finally conceding to Janice and laying down a different card.

"I want to be normal."

She blinked rapidly at me. "Why?"

"I would be in college right now."

"What would you study?" She turned back to the game, laying a black card down this time.

"I wanted to be an artist."

"No one can be an artist," she scoffed. "Unless you're like... who ever that dude was who drew that lady."

Janice rolled her eyes wildly. "Anyone can be an artist, you idiot."

"Don't call me an idiot, *Janice*."

I sighed deeply and sat back in my seat while another argument broke out between my table mates. Maybe Carrie was right and I never would have been able to do art, maybe I would have had to study law or something my dad wanted me to do – but anything would have been better than where I ended up. At least I would have been able to makes some choices about my life. Here, I couldn't even decide when I was hungry or not.

"Normal is overrated," Leslie declared and then took her hand and swept the entire pile of cards off the table.

"MELODY PARKER."

My head jerked at the unfamiliar sound of my full name. My mother called me Melody but everyone here just called me Mellie or Parker. "Yeah?" I almost raised my hand but stopped myself; everyone in the day room was already staring at me.

"Come with me."

I didn't recognize the nurse and I immediately didn't trust her. "Why?"

"Don't go anywhere with her," Leslie hissed in my ear.

"Dr. Matthews wants to talk to you."

"It's not my time to talk to him," my eyes narrowed as I took in her pale cheeks and red rimmed eyes. "I'll just wait here."

"You'll come with me," she insisted, taking a breath that made her chest raise.

"Fine." Abruptly recognizing defeat, I stood up and followed her down the familiar hallways that led to Dr. Matthews' office.

"Come on in, Mellie," he called as soon as he saw me in the small waiting area. There was something in his voice that I didn't like. My heart sped up.

"Why did you want to see me early?" I questioned without preamble.

"Go ahead and sit down." The nurse shut the door but didn't leave the room. Hidden in her hand was a small syringe that she was trying to keep me from seeing.

"What's going on?" I sank, shaking, onto the couch.

"There's been some...news...about Beth," he said slowly.

"Really?" I leaned forward eagerly. "Is she getting out of solitary? Are you moving her or does she get to come back here?"

"Mellie." He took his glasses off and set them down on his desk. "Beth… isn't going to come back here."

"Ok." Disappointment weighed heavily on my shoulders.

"She's… Beth…"

"She's what?"

"It appears that she took her own life yesterday afternoon."

"What?" The room was suddenly loud…too loud for me to hear what he was saying. Next to me, Leslie hissed between her closed teeth. The nurse took a step forward. "I don't understand what you're saying."

"I'm very sorry," Dr. Matthews continued in his same stupidly calm voice. "I know she was your friend. I wanted you to hear this terrible news from me and not in the day room."

"She's dead?" Leslie exploded the entire room. "Is that what you said?"

"Yes."

"How could you let something like that happen?" she screamed, bolting up from the couch. "You were supposed to take care of her, you just let her die like some animal?" The room began to spin while Leslie screamed at Dr. Matthews. The nurse came forward and I knew what she was going to do with that syringe. She didn't need it though; everything was already going dark.

EVEN THOUGH I DIDN'T think I could cry anymore, tears still streamed down my face at an unrelenting pace. Maybe I would never stop crying. They had hooked me up to an IV again – one that forced water into my body. If I never ran out of water, I would never stop crying. But I couldn't summon up enough energy to care that much.

"How could this happen, Leslie?" I asked – again. "She was in room all by herself, how was she able to hurt herself?"

"Cuz this hospital is shit," she growled. "They don't care what happens to any of us."

"It's a prison," I mumbled, correcting her.

"What?" Her narrowed eyes hoovered over my bed.

"You called it a hospital, but it's a prison."

"It's supposed to be a hospital for the criminally insane." Her shoulders raised with her deep breath. "But they don't care."

"They just left her by herself," I whimpered. "They knew she wasn't ok."

"You're not safe here, Mellie," she declared in a soft voice. "I need to keep you safe." Her narrowed eyes widened back out to normal.

"How?"

"Don't worry," she cooed, "you just sleep." Leslie curled her legs under her and sat beside me on the bed. For the first time in a while, I actually did feel better with her near me.

I WAS JOLTED AWAKE by the door creaking open. A small slice of light spilled into the room and washed across my face. I tried to peel my eyes open wide enough to see who was standing at the end of my bed, but the light was too bright. My head stayed flat on the pillow.

"Are you awake?" the person asked harshly.

"Go away," Leslie snarled at her when I didn't say anything. I was glad she answered for me, my tongue felt much too swollen to be able to form any words.

The door clicked shut again, blanketing me in darkness again.

"Just go back to sleep, Mellie," Leslie purred.

Gratefully, I obeyed.

"HOW ARE YOU FEELING, Mellie?" Dr. Matthews asked, clicking his pen open and closed over and over again.

Why did everyone keep asking me that? "Fine," I shrugged.

"I'm relieved to see you out of your room." He was still speaking to me in careful tones.

"It's only been a few days," Leslie snapped. "You can't just expect her to get over what happened to Beth in a day, they were good friends."

"It's been three weeks," he gently corrected her. "Things will be difficult for a while. You may never get over this completely. Getting back into a routine will help..."

Dr. Matthews voice droned on and on but the words stopped making sense. It was easier to just let Leslie talk to him, I didn't want to talk about Beth to him or to anyone else. Three weeks? Time moved differently here but he probably wasn't lying to me. What did I know though?

"DID YOU HEAR WHAT HAPPENED?"

"I guess she killed a nurse."

"Then she killed herself."

The whispers in the day room were too loud. Why did Nurse Kaydee insist that I come in here? This was not *"good for me"*.

"Just ignore them," Leslie suggested.

"I know." With a sigh that started low in my stomach, I let my head fall sideways until it hit the coolness of the window.

"Mellie," Carrie jabbed her finger into my shoulder. "Come play cards, Janice is cheating."

"I don't want to." I brushed her hand away without looking at her.

"Oh come one," she pleaded. "You can't just mope around forever."

"Go away, Carrie," Leslie sneered.

"Whatever." She stuck her middle finger in the air as she made her way back to the table where Janice was waiting.

"I don't want to play cards," I muttered to the glass.

"Don't worry about her." Leslie moved so she could stand directly in front of me. "Don't worry about anyone."

"Med pass," Nurse Kaydee announced, moving Leslie aside so she could hand me the small cup of pills.

"Why are there so many?" Leslie asked sharply. "She only takes three pills."

"Dr. Matthews added some medication. He's hoping it will help you get some of your energy back."

"No." Leslie shook her head firmly.

"These will help, Mellie."

"No way. You're not drugging her up like you did to Beth." Leslie's voice rose.

"Mellie."

"No." In one sudden motion, Leslie swung her hand upwards and knocked the pills out of Nurse Kaydee's hand.

For one second that seemed to last a lot longer, the two of them stared at each other – both glaring. Nurse Kaydee looked away first. "That's it, Parker. Back to your room. Dr. Matthews will hear about this."

"Like she cares," snarled Leslie.

"LESLIE?"

"I'm here."

"Thank you for helping me."

"I'll always help you."

"Will you keep me safe?"

"It's what I'm here for, Mellie."

I let out my deep breath and punched my pillow into a more comfortable mass. "I'm glad you're here, Leslie," I murmured sleepily.

"You just sleep." She pushed the small sprouts of hair off my forehead. "I'll stay right here."

Finally feeling secure, I let my eyelids slide closed.

About the Author

Amy Richie has lived in a small town her entire life. She lives with her three kids and their cats, George and Ellie. She began writing in high school but never took it seriously until a few years ago. She enjoys writing because it takes her out of her everyday life and gives life to the people in her head. "When I was little I wanted to be a mermaid, then when I was in high school I wanted to be a vampire; now as an adult I'm a writer, which is better because now I get to be both."

Read more at amyrichie.weebly.com.